"Mmmm."

Jack made the sound low in his throat as he chewed the chocolate. "I like it. What is the candy called?"

"Heavenly Kisses."

A slow, purely male smile curved his lips. "The taste...the name..." His gorgeous blue eyes darkened with desire as he stared at Kayla's mouth. "It conjures up all kinds of possibilities, don't you think?"

"Try another," she urged breathlessly, aroused by the sexual magnetism that radiated off him.

Kayla had no idea how long it might take for the stimulant to take effect on Jack...but by all appearances, the aphrodisiac seemed to be working fast!

He picked up another piece and bit off half of it, then lifted the remaining half to her mouth, tempting her. "Your turn," he said, and gently slipped the chocolate past her parted lips.

Her tongue touched his finger as she accepted his offering, and he groaned again. She found herself mesmerized by the erotic heat flaring in his eyes. He stepped closer, bringing with him the delicious heat of his body.

"How about we see if that candy of yours lives up to its name?" he whispered just before his lips claimed hers....

Dear Reader,

Have you ever wondered if those advertisements for aphrodisiacs really work? Sprinkle a bit in your food or drink and voilà, you're instantly in the mood? Well, Kayla Thomas, my heroine of *Pure Indulgence*, is curious enough to give it a try and decides to add an aphrodisiac to some very sensual candies she's creating for her bakery shop. And who better to test those candies on than the sexy hero, Jack Tremaine? The results are *very* stimulating....

I hope you enjoy Kayla and Jack's fun, sexy story. I love to hear from my readers, and you can write to me at P.O. Box 1102, Rialto, CA 92377-1102 (send SASE for goodies!) or at janelle@janelledenison.com. Be sure to check my Web site for information on all my upcoming releases at www.janelledenison.com.

Happy reading,

Janelle Denison

Books by Janelle Denison

HARLEQUIN TEMPTATION
799—TEMPTED
811—SEDUCED
832—SEDUCTIVE FANTASY
844—WILD FANTASY
888—A SHAMELESS SEDUCTION

HARLEQUIN BLAZE
12—HEAT WAVES
33—A WICKED SEDUCTION
61—THE ULTIMATE SEDUCTION

Don't miss any of our special offers. Write to us at the following address for information on our newest releases.

Harlequin Reader Service
U.S.: 3010 Walden Ave., P.O. Box 1325, Buffalo, NY 14269
Canadian: P.O. Box 609, Fort Erie, Ont. L2A 5X3

Janelle Denison
PURE INDULGENCE

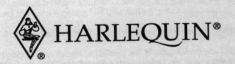

HARLEQUIN®

TORONTO • NEW YORK • LONDON
AMSTERDAM • PARIS • SYDNEY • HAMBURG
STOCKHOLM • ATHENS • TOKYO • MILAN • MADRID
PRAGUE • WARSAW • BUDAPEST • AUCKLAND

To my Plot Monkey Pals, Carly Phillips, Julie Elizabeth Leto and Leslie Kelly. Thank you for great times, phenomenal brainstorming sessions and a special circle of friendship.

To my extraordinary editor, Brenda Chin.
Thank you for your patience, support and understanding.
You are a gem among editors!

And as always, to my husband, Don,
who is my main indulgence...
other than Starbucks, of course! < g >

ISBN 0-373-69147-5

PURE INDULGENCE

Copyright © 2003 by Janelle Denison.

Visit us at www.eHarlequin.com

Printed in U.S.A.

1

"*OH, GOD,*" Jillian moaned in pure, unadulterated ecstasy. "Your triple fudge Bavarian torte is right up there with great sex—not that I've had any of that lately."

Kayla Thomas grinned at her sister's cheeky comment as Jillian sampled another bite of the new dessert Kayla had concocted that morning. "I can barely remember what sex is like, great or otherwise," she replied wryly. "That's how long it's been for me."

"Fortunately, you're surrounded by the next best thing. *Chocolate.*" Jillian waggled her brows in a lascivious manner. "And lucky me, I get to be your official taste tester. This one is a definite winner and gets a five-moan recommendation."

Kayla laughed and continued arranging an assortment of *petits fours* on a silver tray. "Oh good, I'll be sure to put *that* on the packaging label." Thoughtful for a moment, she then added, "Since the torte has your approval, I think I'll include it as one of the desserts for the Chamber of Commerce function I'm catering tonight."

Jillian licked bits of chocolate from her full bottom lip, obviously not wanting to waste even a crumb of the dessert. "You'll have them all salivating for more."

With a smile at her sister's reply, Kayla glanced across the industrial-sized prep table separating them. They were alone in the kitchen area of Pure Indulgence since her two other employees were handling the front counter while Kayla prepared for the Commerce function that evening.

"I'll just be happy if I can drum up a bit of extra catering business," Kayla said.

"I have no doubts that you will." Jillian set her empty plate in the sink, came up beside Kayla, and started putting the small, fancy cakes onto a scalloped paper liner to help speed up the packaging process. "You're doing so great. Look at all that you've accomplished."

Jillian's tone was infused with genuine pride as she swept a quick glance around the back of the shop, taking in the cakes and pastries cooling on bakery racks, and the refrigerators filled with dozens of different desserts. "I always knew you'd be a success in your own right. No other place in San Diego comes close to creating desserts as outstanding as yours."

Kayla appreciated Jillian's support more than she could ever express. Despite a childhood spent with a mother constantly pitting them against one another, they'd managed to remain close. The bond had become even stronger after their mother had passed away and was no longer around to interfere in their lives.

"I learned most of my skills during those summers with Grandma Thomas. She taught me my way around a kitchen and how to bake from scratch," Kayla said fondly. "But *you're* the one that made Pure Indulgence, and all this, possible."

Her sister made a *pfft* sound that Kayla recognized as a dismissal of her gratitude. "I might have helped to get your own bakery shop opened, but *you're* the one who made it solvent after six months' time. I had nothing to do with that."

"You know I can't thank you enough for your help." Financially and emotionally, her sister had been a rock for Kayla the past year.

Jillian's green eyes softened. "It was my pleasure. Truly."

Kayla finished filling the tray and started on another, knowing deep in her heart that Jillian had more to do with her success than she'd ever admit or take credit for. When her sister had retired from her modeling career in New York nearly a year ago and returned to San Diego to start out fresh and new, Kayla had been working during the day as a secretary and spending her nights as a cocktail waitress. She'd been scrimping and saving so she could afford to open a small bakery. While she'd managed to accumulate quite a nest egg, she'd been years away from her goal.

Jillian, who'd made an ungodly amount of money as a cover model, had insisted on giving Kayla the cash she needed to open her bakery. Even after putting away every penny, Kayla would have been able to afford nothing more than a small shop in a run-down grocery center. Her sister had landed her a prime spot in Seaport Village, one of San Diego's most exclusive shopping plazas.

Kayla had been overwhelmed by her sister's generosity and had sworn she'd pay back every last cent, but Jillian wouldn't hear of it. It was a gift, she'd said, so Kayla could finally follow her own dreams.

"You know," Jillian said as she absently bit into a mocha butterball she filched from a nearby tray, "since tonight's function is being held by the Chamber of Commerce, I'm betting there's going to be plenty of single businessmen milling about, which means this could be a ripe opportunity for you to snag a guy and end your run of celibacy."

Kayla rolled her eyes. "Easy for you to say, and not so easy for me to do," she teased.

"It's not so easy for me either," Jillian replied in a guarded tone that Kayla understood all too well.

She watched Jillian polish off the gourmet candy, envying the way her gorgeous, slender sister could put away so many sweets without any weight gain, while all Kayla had to do was inhale the scent of sugar and an extra pound seemed to find its way to her already curvaceous hips. While their naturally blond hair and green eyes were sisterly traits they had in common, that's where the physical resemblance between them ended.

Despite Jillian's successful modeling career, the two of them shared the same self-doubts when it came to men. Kayla, who'd always been compared to her beautiful, thin sister by their mother, was especially self-conscious. Most men judged women by their looks, as Kayla had learned the hard way.

Kayla was softly rounded thanks to the extra twenty pounds she couldn't seem to shed permanently, no matter how hard she tried. In Jillian's case, all men saw were centerfold curves and not the warm, intelligent woman inside who craved the same kind of unconditional acceptance that Kayla did. It amazed Kayla how opposite she and her sister were in stature and appearance, how differently they were raised as children, yet as adults they shared a very common bond because of those contrasts.

When Jillian had returned from New York emotionally shattered after a relationship gone bad, she and Kayla had made a pact that neither of them would ever again compromise their identities to please a man.

Unfortunately, that alliance didn't help to soothe Kayla's more sensual cravings. To make matters worse, her needs had become heightened by the experimental chocolate aphrodisiacs she'd secretly started creating, and sampling. If all went well and she was able to substantiate that the candies did, indeed, boost a person's sex drive, she'd have a surefire seller to add to her current line of desserts.

But in the meantime, with only herself to test those specialty candies, her body and hormones were becoming increasingly stimulated. Just a few bites left her aroused and aching for the touch of a man's hands, the caress of his mouth on her breasts, the heat and friction of his body within hers. It had been much too long since she'd experienced those kinds of sensual intimacies with a man, and she was beginning to wonder if she needed to do something about her long run of abstinence, as her sister had suggested.

Her new creations would provide the perfect opportunity, if she was able to find a man she was attracted to. Based on what her candies did to a person's libido, she'd be able to reap the benefits of a short, fun affair at the same time that she conducted her experiment. Once she proved that her creations met certain criteria, she would be ready to take the candies public.

Shaking off her thoughts for now, she snapped a clear, plastic lid onto the full tray of *petits fours* and retrieved the cut-up fruit and fondue sauces from the refrigerator. She added them to the growing stack of items she planned to take to the banquet tonight. "Tell you what, I'll do my best to check out the unattached businessmen, but I won't make any promises. I'm there to work, Jillian, not troll for men."

Her sister made a playful face. "You know what they say about all work and no play…"

"Yeah, too much play makes the bills pile up and bankruptcy loom like a dark cloud." For good measure, Kayla jabbed her sister in the side where she was ticklish.

"Okay, okay," Jillian relented around breathless laughter. "Just try to keep an open mind while you're working. One of us has to find our Prince Charming and live happily ever after."

They spent the next hour boxing up the rest of the cakes and other desserts, then transferred them into the shop's van that Kayla used for deliveries. Just as Kayla came back into the kitchen after loading up the last of the order, she caught her sister eyeing a plastic container of candies with too much interest.

"Hey, what are these over here?" Jillian asked, slanting Kayla a curious glance.

"They're a new candy I just created." She wiped down the stainless-steel countertops, all the while watching Jillian to make sure she kept her hands to herself. "I'm calling them Heavenly Kisses."

An amused grin tipped the corner of Jillian's mouth. "I love the name. Very sensual. What's in them?"

"Espresso butter cream and caramel covered in

white chocolate." And a secret ingredient that claimed to stimulate lust in the person who consumed it.

"Oh, yum." Enthusiasm deepened Jillian's voice, and before Kayla could stop her, she opened the plastic lid, picked up one of the smooth, creamy-looking candies, and inhaled its scent. "It smells *wonderful*. I bet it tastes just as good." She opened her mouth to take a bite.

Kayla sucked in a quick breath and released it on a long "*noooo!*" At the same moment, she lunged toward her sister, nearly tackling her in her haste to get the candy out of her hand. Thankfully, she managed to extricate the chocolate from her fingers before Jillian could eat it.

Jillian jumped back in startled surprise and frowned at her. "Geez, Kayla, you're acting like that candy is poisoned or something."

Definitely *or something*. Kayla put the candy back into the container and snapped the lid on tight. "Do you have to put *everything* into your mouth?" she asked, unable to tamp her exasperation over her sister's habit of grazing while she was at the bakery. In this case, she would have gotten more than she bargained for.

"Hey, I'm very selective about what goes into this mouth of mine." Jillian's tone was defensive, but the amusement glimmering in her eyes contradicted her indignation.

Kayla ducked her head sheepishly. Undoubtedly her reaction was out of character and extreme, but she'd just saved Jillian's libido from being whipped into a frenzy of need. And she wasn't prepared to let anyone in on her secret just yet—not until she had a chance to test the candies more thoroughly.

She faced her sister again, and summoned an excuse for her odd behavior. "I'm sorry, Jilly. I didn't mean to get so upset. It's just that I'm not ready for anyone to taste these just yet."

Jillian's lip puffed out in a feigned pout that only enhanced how beautiful she was. "And here I thought I was your official taste tester."

Kayla put the candies in her tote bag to take home, so no one else would try to eat them without her knowledge. "I promise you'll get a chance to sample them, just as soon as I'm satisfied with the recipe."

"Oh, all right." Seemingly satisfied with that compromise, Jillian wrapped Kayla in a warm, affectionate hug. The significance of the embrace made Kayla smile. As kids they'd made an agreement that any fight or argument followed by a hug meant all was forgiven. As adults, the wordless pact was still as meaningful as ever.

"Good luck tonight." Jillian grabbed her designer purse and slung it over her shoulder. "Call me later to let me know how things go, okay?"

"I will."

Kayla watched Jillian sashay from the kitchen, and could only shake her head when her sister snatched a Chantilly cream puff from a cooling rack on her way out the back exit.

JACK TREMAINE WAS SEDUCED by her smile. As sweet and addictive as the desserts she was serving, the teasing curve to her sensual mouth lured his attention back to her time and again. Her laughter had the same effect, a husky, playful sound that instigated a spark of desire low in his belly.

The instantaneous response was unlike anything he'd experienced in a very long time, and he was undeniably intrigued by this woman's ability to affect him with nothing more than an impish grin, lilting laughter, and sparkling green eyes. Years of being on the receiving end of so many women's scheming smiles and sly designs of becoming Mrs. Jack Tremaine had obviously jaded him. She was like a breath of fresh spring air.

He took a drink of his cold beer to douse the heat spreading through his veins. He heard the business-related dialogue going on around him but was far more interested in watching the lovely lady interact with the guests than in participating in the conversation. Wearing a uniform of black skirt and white blouse, she moved with natural grace as she served the guests standing in line at the linen-draped dessert table. He assumed she was a waitress employed by the banquet facility hosting the San Diego Chamber of Commerce's Annual Dinner. Despite the plain outfit, there was no denying that she had the kind of sexy, voluptuous body a man could lose himself in for hours, days, *years*. Her breasts were full and soft-looking, definitely more than a generous handful, and her curvaceous hips and long legs were designed to cradle a man in between.

There was nothing dainty, delicate, or overtly sophisticated about her, and that, along with her complete lack of pretense, drew him too.

She glanced up after serving a man a slice of some kind of cheesecake she'd just topped with caramel sauce and whipped cream, and their gazes met and held. She appeared startled to find him staring at her, and the amiable smile on her lips wavered. She even cast a quick, surreptitious look around to make sure that she was the one who'd captured his attention. Then she tipped her head and gave him an uncertain smile.

Before he could continue the silent, flirtatious exchange between them, another guest demanded her attention and the moment was gone. He waited for the line at the table to dissipate, and once she was alone, he excused himself from the group of businessmen and their significant others and headed over to sample a few of the desserts she was offering.

Busy replenishing trays from the portable refrigerator against the wall behind her, she didn't see him approach, giving him the opportunity to appraise her up close. His gaze slid down her backside as she bent low, and he couldn't help but admire the gentle flare of her lush hips, and the way her black skirt tightened very nicely over her shapely bottom, prompting all sorts of sinful, erotic fantasies.

His groin stirred, and he shook himself, hard. Good Lord, he felt like a horny teenager. He'd always preferred real full-bodied figures—and ones that were one-hundred-percent natural. They turned him on much more than the too-thin and artificially enhanced women he'd dated. Their looks were as fake as their interest in him as anything more than a wealthy meal ticket—like his date who'd disappeared to "powder her nose". He'd regretted bringing Gretta even before he'd laid eyes on this woman, and now his feelings were magnified.

For the last few years he'd devoted ninety-nine percent of his attention to making a success of his fine dining restaurant, Tremaine's Downtown, and he'd dedicated one percent to dating. As a result, he'd deliberately gone out with women who wouldn't pose a threat to his time, and who wouldn't affect him emotionally.

But now that his business was financially stable enough for him to open a second restaurant, he was becoming increasingly aware of how much was lacking in his personal life. He realized maybe he was ready to settle down in a committed relationship. He glanced at the woman in front of him and smiled to himself. Obviously he had a whole lot of lost time to make up for.

He hoped for a chance to get to know her before he had to face his date again. And there was no doubt in his mind that he'd be letting Gretta down tonight. Permanently.

The woman turned around with a platterful of fancy candies and came to an abrupt stop. Her green eyes, threaded with gold flecks, widened in surprise, and he could have sworn he heard her suck in a startled breath. Her blond hair was secured into a ponytail away from her girl-next-door pretty face, and she had a beautiful, flawless complexion. His fingers flexed at the urge to reach out and stroke her smooth cheek, to see if her skin was as creamy-soft as it looked.

A slow, lazy grin lifted the corners of his mouth. "You're tempting me," he said huskily. *Boy, was she ever.*

Her gaze turned wary, and she carefully set the silver tray down on the table, causing her blouse to stretch taut across those full, luscious breasts of hers. "Excuse me?"

"You're tempting me...with all these desserts." He waved a hand to encompass the array of confections surrounding him. "I have little to no willpower when it comes to anything sweet."

"Oh." She ducked her head, as if she couldn't quite believe he was flirting with her, but not before he caught the delightful blush sweeping across her cheeks. "What can I get for you?"

Certain the first answer that came to mind would undoubtedly shock her, he decided to behave himself. "Everything looks fabulous. What do you recommend?"

A teasing light entered her eyes. "That all depends on what you're in the mood for."

Oh, man, another loaded question that begged for a suggestive reply. "Let's go with something rich and decadent."

She reached for a plate and slanted him a speculative glance. "Sounds like you've got yourself a major sweet tooth."

He shrugged, and winked at her. "I rarely pass up dessert."

"Ahh, a man after my own heart," she said with a dramatic sigh that was underscored by a mischievous grin, which let Jack know that she was finally relaxing with him. "My personal motto is, 'Life is too short. Eat dessert first'."

He laughed in amusement. "I might have to adopt that motto for myself." He read the place cards in front of each dessert, amazed at the varied and overwhelming selection of treats in front of him. "Hmm, I think I'll try a slice of the chocolate praline layer cake."

She nodded her approval, causing her silky ponytail to swish against her shoulders. He wondered how long her hair was, how the blond strands would feel running through his fingers, trailing across his chest, his belly, his thighs....

"Excellent choice," she said, snapping him out of yet another arousing daydream as she passed him a piece of the decadent-looking cake, along with a fork.

He took a bite, and the silky substance literally dissolved in his mouth. "Oh, wow. This is absolutely delicious."

She looked extremely pleased with his comment. "That's one of my favorites, too, though I have to admit I have too many desserts that I'm fond of," she said a bit sheepishly.

The woman was a mass of intriguing contradictions, from confident to modest in the span of a few moments. But it was those sincere traits that roused his libido and his interest in her. "If everything is as delicious as this, I can see why you have so many favorites." He continued eating his layered cake, and moved down to the end of the table to check out a few pots of melted sauces. "What's this over here?" he asked curiously.

"This is for the more health-conscious," she said wryly, and gestured toward the platter of pineapple wedges, strawberries, peaches, and sliced bananas and apples. "Guests can eat the cut-up fruit just as it is, or for the more adventurous and daring, there's fondue dip."

"I'm definitely feeling adventurous and daring," he said a bit wickedly.

Her gaze glimmered with humor. "In that case, there's Caramel Kahlúa, Chocolate Rum, and Pink Squirrel fondue."

"Pink Squirrel?" he repeated incredulously. "Do I even *want* to know what that consists of?"

She laughed, the light sound pure music to his soul. "Despite the name, it's actually quite good. The dip is made up of marshmallow creme melted with creme d'almond, and creme de cocoa."

He eyed the sauce dubiously. "I suppose I'd look like a wuss if I refused to eat something with such a frou-frou name."

She leaned across the table and placed her hand on his arm in a way that was friendly yet arousing, even through his coat sleeve. "If you don't mind me saying, I don't think anyone could *ever* mistake you for a wuss," she said in a low voice threaded with playful overtures.

He felt his chest expand a few inches beneath his dress shirt, and noticed just how close her glossy lips were. If he lowered his head and moved forward a few inches, he'd have the chance to see if she tasted as good as she looked.

His stomach muscles clenched, and he forced himself to glance away from the temptation of her mouth. He released a taut breath. Oh, man, he was craving her a lot more than the scrumptious confection on his plate—though he was fairly certain she wouldn't appreciate being accosted over the dessert table.

He took another bite of his cake, determined to keep their conversation on track. "You certainly seem to know your desserts."

"I should." She fussed with the assortment of candies, rearranging them on the tray just so, then filled an empty plate with a few different chunks of fruit. "I run my own dessert shop."

"Pure Indulgence?" he guessed.

She stopped stirring the Pink Squirrel fondue, and her gaze jerked to his in startled surprise. "You've been there?"

"No, it's on your name tag." He grinned and pointed his fork at the pin secured on her blouse above her left breast. "As is your name, *Kayla*." Even her name had a soft, seductive ring to it.

"My name tag...of course." She rolled her eyes and shook her head, as if she couldn't believe she'd forgotten the badge that identified her. She poured a small amount of Caramel Kahlúa fondue over the bananas she'd selected for him, and drizzled the squirrel sauce over the strawberries. "Since I don't have the advantage of you wearing a name tag, care to share?"

"Jack Tremaine." She didn't seem to connect his last name to his five-star restaurant, which was more than fine with him for the moment. "It's a pleasure to make your acquaintance." Deliberately, he stretched his hand toward her, giving her little choice but to accept it.

She slipped her warm palm against his much larger one, and he closed his fingers around her slender hand. "It's nice meeting you, too," she said, sounding breathless.

His heartbeat quickened. The sprinkling of gold in her eyes had darkened in awareness, and she dampened her bottom lip with her tongue. There was no denying the chemistry and latent desire that rippled between them, and it was damn nice to know that his interest was reciprocated. He glided his fingers along the soft skin of her wrist, and wished they were alone instead of in a banquet room with two hundred other people.

"Miss," a woman said, diverting Kayla's attention to the other end of the table where an elderly lady was pointing at the small, cut up squares that looked similar to brownies. "What's in these Snicker Brownie Bars?"

Kayla pulled her hand back, and he let her go. "Excuse me while I help this guest," she said to him, seemingly reluctant to abandon his end of the table. She exchanged his finished cake with the plate she'd just prepared for him. "Here, give this fruit and fondue a try. I think you'll like it."

Not ready to leave her just yet, Jack remained where he was and sampled the fruit and different sauces while listening to Kayla as she listed the ingredients of the brownie bars and swayed the older woman to try a small piece.

Absently, his gaze skimmed the table of sweets as he bit into a juicy strawberry topped with the marshmallow cream dip. He'd only sampled a few items so far. Still, he was highly impressed with the wide variety she offered that would please even the most discriminating palate. He was equally swayed by the fact that she'd obviously made the desserts herself.

He popped a sliced banana into his mouth and chewed. As the rich flavor of the Caramel Kahlúa sauce tempted his taste buds, he couldn't help but wonder if the standard desserts he served at Tremaine's Downtown were too ordinary in comparison. It had taken him and his chef years to perfect the main courses and side dishes that blended French cuisine with seafood fare. There was no doubt they had helped to garner a five-star recommendation for his establishment and rave reviews, yet he'd never given much thought to the desserts he'd initially chosen when the restaurant first opened years ago.

Now, he did. Just as he'd spent the time and care refining and improving the entrées at Tremaine's Downtown to a high standard of excellence, maybe it was time to revamp and spruce up the dessert menu, as well. It would be a way to make sure that the final course of the meal lived up to the whole Tremaine's Downtown experience.

"So, what do you think of the fondue?" Kayla was back, her expression expectant as she waited anxiously for his answer. "The Pink Squirrel especially?"

"Incredible," he stated with honest enthusiasm, and licked a smear of Caramel Kahlúa from his thumb. "All of it, and *especially* the pink squirrel."

"See, you aren't a wuss at all," she teased as her dancing eyes drifted to a spot just below his lower lip. "But you do have a bit of the sauce right below your mouth."

He swiped at his chin with the back of his hand. "Did I get it?"

"Ahh, no..." Tentatively, she reached out and removed the sticky substance in a slow caress of her thumb. If it were just the two of them, he would have grabbed her wrist and sucked the sweetness right off her finger, and nibbled and tasted his way up her arm from there.

"See?" She showed him the smear of white froth, a smile in her eyes and on her lips. "That's why only the adventurous should attempt to eat the Pink Squirrel fondue. It can be quite messy."

"Maybe next time you'll just have to feed it to me so I can avoid the mess." That adorable blush swept across her cheeks again, and he had to stifle an amused laugh. "So, tell me, do you make all these desserts, cakes and candies from scratch?"

She grabbed a napkin to wipe her sticky finger and nodded. "Using only the finest, freshest ingredients, of course."

Judging by the tastes he'd encountered, he didn't doubt that in the least, which made his interest in her twofold. "And where is your shop located?"

"Seaport Village," she said, naming one of San Diego's biggest and most popular landmarks for tourist shopping. "Pure Indulgence has been there for about six months now."

Finished with his fruit and fondue, he handed her the empty plate, which she put in the plastic bin of dirty dishes behind her. "Have you ever heard of Tremaine's Downtown?"

"Of course I have. You can't live in San Diego and not have heard of the restaurant, though I've never been there myself." She refilled the fork and napkin holders, keeping busy as she talked. "But if you're looking for a recommendation, I hear the food and service there are outstanding."

He pushed his hands into the front pockets of his trousers. "So I've been told a time or two."

She blinked at him, momentarily confused by his comment, then understanding dawned. "Ohmigosh, Tremaine's Downtown is *your* restaurant?"

"Yep. And I was thinking, after trying your desserts and seeing that there's more out there than chocolate mousse and plain cheesecake, it's time I update my dessert menu. Make it more exotic and different, rather than just offering the same old thing that everyone else does."

"Updating is always a good thing," she agreed. "As is offering your dining customers something different and unique to your restaurant alone."

"Exactly," he said, pleased that she concurred with his way of thinking. "Do you accept custom orders? Such as creating one-of-a-kind desserts that could be exclusive to Tremaine's Downtown alone?"

Her eyes widened, and she placed a hand on her chest. "You want *me* to design your desserts?"

Her tone was incredulous, her expression so awed that he wanted to laugh, but instead he nodded seriously. "Yes, I do."

"Oh, wow," she breathed in amazement. "I've never had anyone ask for an exclusivity agreement before, but in this case, it can certainly be arranged."

"Excellent." That's precisely what he wanted to hear, and he experienced a rush of anticipation over the thought of giving his dessert menu an overhaul, especially with his new restaurant, Tremaine's Uptown, being built within the next year. And it didn't hurt that he'd be in close contact with Kayla and could get to know her better. "Do you have a business card with you?"

"Actually I do." Withdrawing a card from her pocket, she handed it to him from across the table. "I never leave home without them."

Another brush of their fingers sent a surge of awareness rippling between them. He caught the flash of heat and desire in her dark gaze, and felt the intimate connection that teased them both with an abundance of possibilities. It was an attraction he intended to pursue, right along with sampling more of her decadent desserts.

"This is great, Kayla Thomas." He tucked the business card into his inside coat pocket for safekeeping. "You'll definitely be hearing from me."

Their eyes met and held, her mouth curving into that soft, sensual smile of hers that too easily wreaked havoc on his libido. "I'm looking forward to it," she said, her voice husky.

"Jack, *darling*, there you are!"

Jack stiffened at the high-pitched, overly possessive sound of his date's voice interrupting his too-short interlude with Kayla. Reality intruded with an unpleasant jolt, and he reluctantly turned to find Gretta Ward fast approaching on her stiletto heels. The other woman eyed Kayla with disdain before she came up to Jack's side, hooked her arm through the crook of his elbow, and pressed her silicone-enhanced breasts and lithe, slender body against his.

His gut clenched hard as he watched the hopeful smile fade from Kayla's lips. Disappointment etched her features, and he knew she'd come to the conclusion that Gretta was his girlfriend and everything that had transpired between them had been a flirtatious farce. She likely thought he'd been toying with her like some kind of insensitive jerk. Of course that was far from the truth, but there was no way to explain the situation without making a bigger mess of things.

Gretta pouted up at him, her sulky expression adding to the dramatic display. "I've been looking for you for the past fifteen minutes."

She scolded him in a way that made him feel like a small child, which grated on his nerves, as did most of Gretta's antics. Over the years, he'd gotten into the habit of dating convenient women, and he didn't realize how much they bored and disgusted him, until now.

Very calmly, he replied. "You disappeared off to the ladies' room, and while you were gone I thought I'd try out the desserts."

Gretta wrinkled her nose at the assortment of cakes, candies and other treats, then brazenly slipped her hand inside his coat and smoothed her palm over his chest in a blatant display of ownership. "I'm the only sweet thing you need, darling."

He inwardly cringed and tried to disengage her from his arm to give himself breathing room. Like a leech, she refused to let go. "The fruit and fondue are great. You ought to give it a try."

"I'll pass." Gretta slanted a quick, assessing glance toward Kayla. "I work hard at keeping my figure in shape, and that means watching what I eat."

While Gretta's tone was casual, her words sounded too much like a deliberate slur against Kayla's softer, fuller curves. And judging by the quick flash of pain he saw in Kayla's eyes, followed closely by her physical withdrawal, he knew Gretta's comment had struck a vulnerable nerve.

"Besides," Gretta went on, dismissing Kayla in favor of returning her attention to Jack, "you know I don't eat anything made from refined sugar and that fondue is no doubt filled with sugar and carbohydrates."

No, he didn't know that about her, and her attempt at familiarity in front of Kayla annoyed him. Though by the calculating look in Gretta's eyes, she'd probably watched them from afar and was purposefully goading Kayla while staking her claim on him.

Of which she had none, he thought irritably.

After three dates with Gretta, and especially after tonight, it was becoming increasingly obvious that it was time to sever their relationship before she entrenched herself any deeper into his life. Each of the three times they'd been together, she grew more smothering, more demanding, and now, too damned possessive. The signs were ones he recognized too well—like many that had come before Gretta, she had designs on becoming Mrs. Jack Tremaine.

Not likely. She was far from what he considered wife material, which made him look at Kayla in a whole new light.

The contrast between the two women was glaring. While Gretta was outwardly beautiful and sophisticated with an amazing body compliments of plastic surgery, she lacked the warmth and genuine goodness that Kayla exuded so effortlessly, so naturally. And those traits were beginning to matter to him, in ways he was more than ready to open himself up to. With the right woman.

A man and his wife came up to the table, and Kayla quietly excused herself to help the couple choose their desserts. But not before he saw the regret glimmering in her eyes.

He felt like the world's biggest heel.

He wanted to call her back, apologize for Gretta's rude comments, and explain that his interest in her was real. But there was nothing left to say to Kayla...not until he ended things with Gretta.

Which couldn't be soon enough for him.

2

"So, HOW DID your catered event go tonight?"

"Not bad." Tucking the cordless phone between her neck and ear, Kayla settled against the pillows propped against the headboard of her bed, glad to hear her sister's encouraging voice after her busy, exhausting evening. "Better than expected, actually." *If you don't count what an absolute fool I made of myself over the gorgeous, sexy Jack Tremaine.*

She cringed at the embarrassing memory, still unable to believe that she'd read all the signals between them so inaccurately. She'd thought, *hoped,* that the attraction was mutual, that the interest she'd glimpsed in the depths of his devastatingly blue eyes had been real.

Obviously, she'd only imagined what she *wanted* to be real—for her to be the focus of a good-looking man's attentions, and for him to look deeper than at surface appearances.

The truth of the matter was, she wasn't head-turningly gorgeous or sophisticated, and she never would be. That wasn't who she was, as she'd learned the hard way in her previous relationship.

Doug had been a good-looking man she'd met after struggling to shed those stubborn twenty pounds that always seemed to hang on to her hips and thighs. They'd dated for a year, and she'd thought he might be "the one", until she'd gradually started gaining the weight back. Then, she'd seen a very judgmental side to the man she'd thought she'd known so well. That side had reinforced every negative comment her mother had ever made about her less-than-perfect body. Doug had issued her an ultimatum that had struck right where she was the most vulnerable—get skinny again, or get dumped.

Knowing she was destined to be curvaceous, and refusing to change for any man ever again, she'd ended the relationship. It had taken her months to come to terms with the fact that she'd never be svelte and slender like her sister, to believe in herself and accept her full curves and ordinary, but pretty features. She only had relapses when someone or something dredged up the insecurities she'd lived with most of her life.

And Jack Tremaine's date had managed to do that exceptionally well.

"Did you dazzle the Chamber of Commerce members with your awesome desserts?" Jillian asked, pulling her back from her unpleasant memories.

"I had no complaints." And that was enough for Kayla to consider the evening a victory. "A few chamber members took my business card for future events, so, all in all, it was great exposure." Though it remained to be seen if any of them actually followed up on their promises to contact her—especially Jack Tremaine.

"Here comes the million-dollar question. Did you meet any good-looking businessmen this evening?" Jillian's tone was low and teasing.

Kayla's cheeks flushed at the one man in particular who loomed larger than life in her mind, and she closed her eyes to bring him into better focus. Too easily, she conjured up seductive blue eyes that set her pulse fluttering, pitch-black hair cut into a short, executive style that accentuated his chiseled features, and big hands with long, tapered fingers designed to bring a woman's body immense pleasure. Then there was that sexy, lean frame of his that filled out his charcoal suit as if it had been custom made for him—and no doubt probably had.

She bit her bottom lip and pressed a hand to the butterflies taking flight in her stomach, debating whether or not to share her secret with Jillian. She was dying to confide in someone about Jack Tremaine, and Jillian was not only her sister, but one of her best friends.

"Okay, so I did meet a guy," Kayla said on a rush of breath. "And I have to confess that he looked more scrumptious than that triple fudge Bavarian torte you were eating earlier today."

"Whoa!" Jillian's breezy laughter drifted over the

phone line. "I didn't think anything topped that dessert!"

Kayla giggled, too, and added naughtily, "I wanted to top *him* with the dessert and eat him up, bite by delicious bite."

"You are *so* bad," Jillian scolded lightly, though she was enjoying their playful banter just as much. "Is he single and available?"

Her little fantasy of having Jack Tremaine covered in her richest, most mouthwatering torte came to a screeching halt. "Unfortunately, no. After he spent a good fifteen minutes flirting with me, this svelte young woman on stiletto heels came along, hooked her arm possessively through his and glared at me. I think if I'd dared to touch him, she'd have clawed my eyes out."

Kayla still found it hard to believe she'd misjudged Jack Tremaine so badly, that she'd let his charming words suck her in. The other woman hadn't seemed at all his type intellectually, neither had her cool personality. But then again, his lady friend had the kind of Barbie-doll shape that turned a man's head. And sometimes men found outward beauty more attractive than brains.

"What can I say," she said, striving for a flippant tone that she didn't completely feel. "Some girls have all the luck, and the figure to go with it."

"Kayla..." Jillian said softly.

"I'm okay. Really," she assured her sister, and directed their conversation back to business. "The guy I met is Jack Tremaine, who owns Tremaine's Downtown. He said he was interested in revamping his dessert menu and took my business card, but it remains to be seen if he'll actually call."

"Wow, Kayla, that would be quite a name to add to your résumé."

"Tell me about it," she said wryly, and gave her sister the details of her conversation with Jack. Then she brought their call to an end with a promise to meet her for lunch later in the week.

Once Kayla hung up the phone, she tried to fall asleep. It was late and she was exhausted, yet peaceful slumber eluded her. She tossed and turned restlessly as Jack Tremaine starred in her most erotic fantasies, and her silk and lace chemise slid arousingly across her breasts, her stomach, and thighs.

With a low groan of frustration, she got up, grabbed her matching robe, and slipped into the silky garment. Some women went gaga over purses or shoes, but pretty lingerie was Kayla's one weakness over chocolate. And because she wore plain, loose clothing in public that didn't draw any attention to her body, in private she indulged that sensual, feminine side of herself freely and without guilt.

She padded barefoot into the kitchen and was greeted by her orange tabby-cat, Pumpkin, who'd ap-

peared on her doorstep last Halloween as a stray and
had made Kayla's home her own since then.

Bending down, she scratched Pumpkin behind her
ears, which triggered an automatic rumbling sound
deep in the cat's throat. "Hi, purry-bug," Kayla murmured affectionately. "Are you looking for a late-night
snack, too?"

"*Mrroww*," the cat replied.

"I thought so." Smiling, Kayla gave the tabby a few
cat treats, then poured herself a glass of milk. She set a
few of the espresso butter cream candies she'd brought
home with her on a plate. She hadn't had a chance to
sample them earlier because of her busy schedule getting the desserts ready for the Chamber of Commerce
dinner.

Sitting at the small dining table, she took a bite of her
newest aphrodisiac creation, and the combined ingredients of espresso, caramel and rich, smooth white
chocolate literally melted in her mouth. Amazingly,
there was no odd aftertaste of the aphrodisiac powder
that she'd purchased on a whim from a new-age Web
site that catered to the mystical and magical. The all-
natural stimulant was said to increase and enhance a
person's sexual response when consumed, and so far,
Kayla found that claim to be true.

After eating three of the Heavenly Kisses candies she
knew she had to stop or her body would be feverish
with need and her night would be even more agoniz-

ing. Already, that familiar tingling sensation was spreading through her veins, making her feel warm all over. Her breasts grew heavy and sensitive, her nipples hardened, and a slow, steady ache spiraled low.

She took a big gulp of cold milk, but knew from previous samplings that it was too late to douse her growing desire, the stripping away of her inhibitions, or the slow building need for an orgasm. But beyond her body's aroused state, she was excited by the possibility that she'd hit upon a unique addition to add to her growing selection of confections. She imagined a whole new line of desserts, all designed to arouse a lover's passion, and she couldn't wait to offer such a fun, sexy item on her bakery menu.

Oh, yeah, she thought with a naughty grin, and licked the lingering flavor of caramel and white chocolate from the corner of her mouth. But before she could make that claim, there was other data she needed to analyze, such as how long it took after eating the candies to become stimulated and what different levels of arousal they could create.

At this point, she only had her own physical responses to go by, and it wasn't enough to come to any kind of solid conclusion. She had to test her candies on an unsuspecting person, someone without any kind of precontrived notions. She needed that tangible proof that her enticing creations ignited a man's sexual appetite as much as it did hers.

But who to use as a guinea pig for her experiment? One man in particular immediately came to mind, and she wouldn't have hesitated to use him for her research—if he wasn't already taken. That left her choices quite limited, and she wasn't about to use her aphrodisiacs on just anyone.

She sighed. As for tonight, she was on her own to deal with her body's demands, so she did the only thing she could. She returned to bed and took her fantasies of Jack Tremaine with her.

FIVE DAYS AFTER the Commerce dinner, Jack still couldn't get Kayla Thomas off his mind, and like a man driven by a deep burning need, he *had* to see her again. Thoughts of her had consumed him during the day when he should have been concentrating on the proposals and estimates he needed to review and approve for the new restaurant. Those thoughts had followed him right into some pretty intense erotic dreams. Each morning he'd awakened with an aching hard-on, and a cold shower had been a lousy substitute for what he really wanted—the reality of Kayla, soft and warm beneath him.

The image of that provocative fantasy had the fly of his jeans growing uncomfortably tight as he drove toward Seaport Village, reminding him just how long he'd been without a woman.

He'd never slept with Gretta and had ended things

with her the night of the dinner, which had resulted in her slamming her door in his face. But her scorn was a small price to pay for his freedom. With new and exciting prospects beckoning to him, he felt more charged and alive than he had in months, possibly years. Tremaine's Downtown was getting a new dessert menu, and now he was completely free to explore his attraction to Kayla.

Jack turned into the Seaport Village parking lot, parked his Escalade, and headed to the directory in front of the shops. He found a listing for Pure Indulgence and followed the map to her place of business, which was located between a wind-chime store and an art gallery.

He stepped inside the bakery shop and was immediately embraced by the delicious fragrance of sweet confections and baked goods. It was after six in the evening, yet the place was impressively packed with customers waiting their turn to order from the glass displays filled with an array of cakes, cookies, candies, and other treats. Two young girls worked quickly and efficiently behind the counter, but Kayla was nowhere in sight.

It would serve him right if she wasn't there, since he hadn't called ahead to make an appointment. But instead of planning a meeting with her, which seemed impossible with his schedule lately, he'd grabbed the first free moment he'd had in days, and before anything else could demand his attention, he'd headed toward Seaport Village.

After a few minutes of waiting for the crowd to thin, he caught the attention of one of the workers and motioned her over. "Excuse me, is Kayla Thomas here?"

The girl eyed him curiously. "Did you have an appointment to see her?" she asked, though her cautious tone told him she didn't think it was likely.

The woman obviously thought he was selling something, when in fact he'd be buying. But he understood the woman's hesitation, as well as her loyalty in protecting her boss from unwanted solicitors. "She should be expecting me," he replied easily, and with just enough assertiveness to sound confident that Kayla would agree to see him. "Tell her it's Jack Tremaine."

"Let me see if she's available," she said, then disappeared through a swinging door that led to a back kitchen area.

Kayla was immersed in accounting paperwork in her office when her full-time employee, Sarah, knocked lightly on her open door, then stepped inside.

"Do you need help out front?" Kayla asked automatically.

From six to seven during the week was the shop's busiest time, when tourists wanted a sweet treat before heading back to their hotels, and locals stopped in to buy their families' favorite dessert on their way home from work. Kayla was always prepared to step in and help at the front counter if necessary.

"It's the normal six o'clock rush, but we've got it under control," Sarah assured her. "Actually, there's a man here who asked to see you. His name is Jack Tremaine, and he said you were expecting him?"

Just the mere mention of Jack's name was enough to send an unexpected warmth spreading through Kayla's veins, not to mention a good dose of shock. After five days of not hearing from him, she'd convinced herself that he hadn't been serious about his interest in revamping his dessert menu. She'd also considered the possibility that he'd found a more experienced, well-known company to handle the job instead of taking a risk with a small, up-and-coming bakery.

She'd finally come to terms with that probability, and now here he was, asking for her—and she was nowhere near prepared to see him again. Not mentally, anyway. She felt thrown off balance, and she didn't care for the bit of hope scratching below the surface of her shock.

She took a deep breath in an attempt to regain her composure, and said to her employee, "Give me a minute, and I'll be right out."

Once Sarah was gone, Kayla stood and made a quick trip to the rest room. As she was washing her hands, she caught sight of her reflection in the mirror and cringed. Good Lord, she looked a mess. Then again, she had spent most of the day elbow-deep in flour and sugar.

She took off her stained apron, but there were a few smudges of chocolate on her baggy T-shirt that she couldn't do much about. As for her hair, wispy strands had escaped her ponytail and there were sugar granules on her cheek. She wiped them away with her hand. She didn't wear much makeup, but what she had put on that morning was nearly gone. She found herself opening the medicine cabinet over the sink and using the colored, flavored lip gloss she kept in there to keep her lips from getting dry and chapped.

She made a sound of disgust at herself for even primping that much for Jack Tremaine. He wasn't there to seduce her, for crying out loud, and she had no desire to try and impress him. Okay, so that was a blatant lie, but what he saw was what he got—a woman who worked hard for a living and had no qualms about looking the part.

With a decisive nod, and determined to be all business this time with Jack Tremaine, she headed out to the front of the shop.

Broad-shouldered and a good six inches taller than any of her customers, all of which at the moment were female, she was able to spot him immediately. He was standing by one of the display cases, checking out the goods and conversing with a few of her customers who no doubt were drawn to his good looks and disarming grin.

He'd obviously asked about their favorite Pure Indulgence desserts, because the older, gray-haired woman next to him was raving about the Boston Cream pies and custard tarts, while another patron chimed in about how fantastic the lemon cheesecake bars were.

He thanked them for their opinions, and reached out to take a sample from the tray on the counter that she always kept filled with bite-size pieces of the previous day's desserts so her customers could try something new before purchasing the item. It was amazing how many extra sales she generated due to that platter of tidbits, and those samples had become one of her best forms of advertising.

Jack tossed a generous chunk of baked apple crisp into his mouth, then turned around to find her standing behind him. He came to an abrupt stop, his vivid blue eyes widening ever so slightly, making him look like a little boy who'd just been caught with his hand in the cookie jar. Except, other than the impish grin curving the corner of his sensual lips, there was nothing boyish about him.

She didn't think it possible, but the man was even sexier and more gorgeous than she remembered, and she supposed his casual attire was partly responsible for making him look so damned tempting. Unlike the suit he'd worn the other night, the collared shirt he wore accentuated his wide chest and flat belly, and well-worn jeans gave her a perfect view of his narrow hips and long, powerful-looking legs. His body was athletically honed, strong and lean and all male, and built to make a woman entertain all kinds of lascivious, sinful thoughts. The man was dangerous, potent stuff.

"Hi, there," he said once he had the chance to swallow his mouthful of apple crisp.

"I'm glad to see you're enjoying the samples," she said, more amused than she wanted to be by his natural, easygoing charm.

"I couldn't help myself." His sultry grin matched the deep, velvet-edge timbre of his voice. "I told you the other night that I have little willpower when it comes to anything sweet."

So he had, though his words today sounded like a seductive warning directed toward *her*. His vibrant gaze drifted to her lips, as if contemplating just how sweet *she'd* taste, and a tremor of awareness rippled through her.

Damn her traitorous body, anyway, she thought, and crossed her arms over her chest to cover the telltale sign of her tight nipples pressing against the front of her shirt. "Be careful, you wouldn't want to overdose on sugar."

"I doubt that's possible," he murmured in bemusement. "But, man, what a way to go."

She almost laughed, then caught herself. He was flirting with her again, and as much as she enjoyed being on the receiving end of his teasing banter, the last she'd seen he had a girlfriend and had no business swapping innuendoes with her.

Business, Kayla. Keep your mind on business, she reminded herself sternly. Since he was the one who'd come to her shop, she waited patiently for him to explain why.

But instead of stating the reason for his presence, he tipped his head and studied her with too much insight. "You look a little surprised to see me."

"Pleasantly surprised, if that makes you feel any better," she said, wondering how this man managed to see beyond her attempt to be professional and composed around him. "I'll admit I wasn't sure whether or not I'd hear from you again."

His gaze caught and held hers steadily. "There's one thing you ought to know about me right up front. I'm a man of my word, and I don't ever say anything that I don't mean or that I don't follow through on."

His tone was adamant, his eyes honest, and she believed him. "That's good to know."

He nodded succinctly. "I know I probably should have called first to let you know I was stopping by, but I was able to get away from the restaurant tonight and took a chance on you being here."

He cast a quick glance around the shop, and while

the initial rush had died down, there were still half a dozen customers waiting to place their orders. "Is this a bad time to talk? Because if it is, I can make an appointment and come back later."

She appreciated his consideration, and her resistance toward him softened a notch. There was no reason to postpone the appointment. Besides, she was curious to find out what he wanted, and if he was still interested in her services. No sense postponing the inevitable.

"Now is fine," she said, and could have sworn she heard him exhale a sigh of relief. "Come on back to my office where we can talk privately."

He followed her through the kitchen, his gaze taking in the wall-to-wall convection ovens, the abundance of cooling racks and proof boxes, and the industrial-size dough-and-batter-mixing machines.

"This is quite a setup you have," he commented, seemingly intrigued by the high-tech equipment she used to create her desserts in mass quantities. "I had no idea you had such a production line back here."

She tossed a smile over her shoulder at him. "It sure does beat doing it the old-fashioned way of mixing and baking one dessert at a time."

He laughed, the low, husky sound touching her in intimate places. "I'm sure it does."

They entered her office, and she took the comfortable tweed chair behind her desk and expected him to take one of the seats in front of her. Instead, he boldly strolled around to where she was sitting, propped his fine backside against the corner of her desk, and crossed one ankle over the other.

The pose was predominantly male, and her pulse leapt at his shameless self-assurance and close proximity. She forced herself to keep her gaze on his handsome face and his sinful blue eyes, but out of her peripheral vision she could see the way his hard, muscular thighs stretched his faded Levi's and she couldn't miss the impressive bulge beneath the fly of his jeans. He was near enough to touch, tempting her to do just that, and it was all she could do to keep her hands to herself when she envisioned pushing him back on her desk and having her wicked way with him.

That burning, aching need she'd been fighting for days now made itself known once again, overwhelming her mind and body with a desire that pulled at her like a riptide. She swallowed a groan. Boy, she had it bad and probably should lay off the aphrodisiac candies, which seemed to have increased her sexual cravings even long after the effects of the stimulant should have worn off—which was a reaction she'd be sure to make note of later. Better yet, she needed to find a sexy, *available* guy to eat her creations, then release all his lust on her.

Oh, yeah, she could definitely go for having her own boy toy for a while. A guy whose sole purpose was to make her body sing with pleasure—over and over again. Especially if he had pitch-black hair, eat-me-up blue eyes, and a mouth made for sin.

Just like the man sitting in front of me.

Another rush of heat swept through her. Drawing a deep breath, she shoved those provocative thoughts right out of her mind before they got her in big trouble.

She leaned back in her chair, putting distance between them any way she could. "So, what can I do for you, Mr. Tremaine?"

"It's Jack, please," he insisted, "especially since we'll be working together."

She raised a brow at his presumptuousness. "We will?"

"I told you I was interested in having you design the desserts for Tremaine's Downtown, and you promised me an exclusivity agreement." He tipped his head questioningly. "Have you changed your mind?"

He looked a little anxious as he waited for her reply, and she found it hard to believe that such a confident man might be worried that she'd refuse his request. Not that she'd pass up such a golden opportunity, but it was nice to know that her agreement mattered to him, that he truly wanted *her* to create his desserts. It gave her a sense of feminine power that was foreign to her, but one she liked very much.

"No, I haven't changed my mind," she said softly, and immediately saw his shoulders relax. "And I'm glad you didn't either."

He graced her with another one of his breathtaking grins. "Then I guess that makes us even."

Yes, it did, and she smiled back at him. "Do you have any preference on the kind of desserts you want?"

"That's what I'm paying you for. To be creative and to provide a variety of different desserts. I'm completely open to new experiences and ideas, so don't hold back."

"It's good to know you're so daring," she teased. "That gives me a whole lot of creative license."

His eyes sparkled just as humorously. "Hey, I tried the Pink Squirrel the other night, didn't I?"

She laughed at his indignant tone. "And you liked it, too," she reminded him.

"That goes to show you the kind of risk-taking guy I can be, so bring it on, sweetheart." He winked at her.

Bring it on. He had no idea just how adventurous her desserts could get, and she couldn't stop herself from wondering what would happen if she mixed a bit of pleasure with their business. The result would be spontaneous combustion, no doubt.

"When do you think you'll have the first dessert ready for me to try?" he asked.

"Let's see," she said thoughtfully, as she opened the day planner on her desk and skimmed through the pages. "It's Wednesday and I need a few days to experiment with some new recipes, and to see what I can come up with. I could have something ready for you to sample, say, by Sunday?"

"That works for me. What time?"

"Since I'd prefer that we weren't interrupted by business, how about six-thirty in the evening, a half hour after the shop closes?"

"Perfect. I'll be here."

She penciled in the appointment on her calendar, and as she did so, her arm brushed his jean-clad hip. She valiantly tried to ignore the heat of him, along with the tightening of her breasts that the chaste touch evoked. She could only imagine the sparks they'd ignite if they ever rubbed skin to skin.

He moved off her desk, straightened, and reached into his back pocket to withdraw his wallet. He pulled a check from his billfold and set it in front of her. She glanced from the staggering amount on the check, all the way back up to his deep, drown-in-them-forever blue eyes.

"What's this for?"

"A down payment for your services," he said matter-of-factly.

"I'd rather wait until services have been rendered and I have a better idea of what you owe." She pushed the check back towards him. "You don't even know if you'll like the desserts I create."

"Then we'll just have to keep working at it until I'm completely satisfied." He didn't seem at all bothered by that possibility. "Besides, I have no doubt you're worth every penny and you'll give me my money's worth. I also know that exclusivity doesn't come cheap."

No, it didn't, but talk about blind trust in her abilities. She shook her head, certain any further argument would be futile. "Okay, fine." If his bill was less than what he'd just given her, she'd issue him a refund. But, boy, would all that money look good in her business account.

"So we have ourselves a deal?"

Since he was towering over her, she stood, too. There was one issue she needed to address before she had her lawyer draw up a final contract and deliver it to Jack. "There's something I need to ask you."

He slid his fingers into the front pockets of his jeans. "Sure. Go ahead."

She didn't know an easy or tactful way to express her concern, so she just let it out. "I got the distinct impression at the Commerce dinner that your girlfriend wouldn't be too thrilled to find out we're working together. Is she going to be a problem for me?" The last thing Kayla wanted or needed was a jealous woman bad-mouthing Pure Indulgence and ruining her hard-earned reputation.

"I broke things off with Gretta the night of the dinner," he told her, and there was no regret in his voice.

"So there's no girlfriend or significant other for you to worry about. I'm single and unattached."

That revelation pleased her, more than was prudent, and she couldn't stop the secretive smile that curved her lips. She'd just found the perfect test subject for her aphrodisiac desserts.

3

JACK WALKED INTO the kitchen area of his restaurant, a last check to make sure that everything was in order before he headed over to Pure Indulgence for his appointment with Kayla. It was fairly busy for a Sunday night, but thanks to his manager and well-trained staff there were no huge problems for Jack to worry about.

A steady stream of appetizers and dinner orders lit up the computer screen of the fully integrated system he'd purchased a few months ago, which kept the kitchen organized and his employees efficient. Behind the warming station his head chef made sure that the cooks processed and prepared the entrées at a steady pace, and still produced the high quality and visually appealing dishes that Tremaine's Downtown was known for.

Satisfied that all was running smoothly, he headed toward his manager, Rich, who was helping to garnish plates and double-checking the dishes before the waiters and waitresses served them to their customers.

Rich wasn't only his right-hand man since Tremaine's Downtown opened six years ago. They'd grown up together in the same impoverished neighborhood and Rich had been his best friend since the age of ten. The two of them had both lost their fathers early on and were raised by single mothers who'd scraped to make ends meet. They'd also been two rebels with plenty of cause, but instead had channeled their energy and young ambition and made something of their lives. He shuddered to think how easily they could have gone the other way.

The two of them had been through a lot together, and managed to remain as close as brothers, supporting one another in everything they did. Jack couldn't imagine his life without Rich in it.

"I'm taking off for the night," Jack said as he came up to his best friend. "Do you need me for anything else before I leave?"

"Nope. I have everything covered just fine." Rich slanted him an inquisitive look as he handed a waitress a dish she was reaching for, taking in Jack's casual shirt and khaki pants, instead of the suit and tie he normally wore when he was working at the restaurant. "Where are you off to? Hot date tonight?"

"No." Not yet, anyway, Jack thought. Kayla definitely made him feel hot and bothered, but despite their mutual attraction, she'd erected a barrier between them that he was determined to gradually break down. As for a date, he hoped that would come in time, as well.

"You know the woman I mentioned who is updating our dessert menu?" Jack asked, reminding Rich of his plans. "I'm meeting with her tonight at her shop."

"And you get to sample her desserts?" he asked slyly. "Sounds like a fun way to spend the evening."

Jack grinned. "I'm not complaining."

Rich's sandy-blond eyebrows rose in surprise. "Do I detect some interest there?"

"Yeah, you do," Jack admitted.

His good friend let out a long, low whistle. "It's been a long time since *you've* been interested in a woman, instead of the other way around."

Jack understood exactly what Rich was getting at, along with the significance of his interest in a woman. He'd almost given up hope in finding a woman who didn't have a hidden agenda where he was concerned, until Kayla, who wasn't at all impressed by who he was, or by his success.

He felt on equal footing with her—personally and professionally—and it was a novel sensation he liked a whole lot.

"She's not like all the other women I've dated." Kayla was intelligent, quick-witted and amusing, with an underlying sensuality that intrigued him from the first moment he'd met her, and continually drew him in deeper with each meeting. But there was no telling how things would progress between them, or if she'd act on the attraction that burned hot and bright whenever they were near one another.

Jack most definitely intended to find out.

"Right now I'm seeing her for business purposes," he told Rich, trying to be pragmatic about the situation. "But we'll see what happens."

The orders into the kitchen picked up, and Jack left the restaurant before he was late for his meeting with Kayla. He made it to her shop with five minutes to spare and knocked on the front glass door, which was locked against any last-minute Sunday-evening shoppers.

She came out of the back room and made her way around the counter to the door. Today she was wearing a pale blue T-shirt that looked a size too big, but didn't do much to hide her generous breasts, if that was her intent. The long hem ended at her thighs, covering a good portion of her body, and from there stonewashed denim took over. Despite the less-than-figure-flattering outfit, her hips swayed sensually as she walked—a direct contrast to her sensible and discreet choice of clothing.

She opened the door, her friendly but shy smile telling Jack she was glad to see him.

"Hi," she said huskily, her warm green gaze filled with a slow, simmering awareness he felt thrum through his blood, as well.

"Hi, yourself," he murmured in reply, and wondered how in the hell he was going to keep his hands off her tonight. He wanted to kiss her in the worst way, wanted to release that clip holding her blond hair on top of her head and sift his fingers through the silky-looking strands. He ached to feel exactly how she fit against him—from her soft breasts, her belly, to her thighs—and everywhere else in between.

Before he followed through on those fantasies dancing in his head, he stepped past her, into the fragrant bakery, and she locked the door behind him.

"Come on back to the kitchen," she said, immediately all business. Then she said over her shoulder as she led the way, "I just perfected your new recipe this morning, and I hope you're happy with the end results."

She was nervous about that, he could tell, and he attempted to set her at ease. "I'm sure you did a great job on the dessert."

"There's always a certain flavor or taste that someone doesn't like, such as coconut, or a citrusy tang, or nuts. For me it's the taste of gingerbread," she said, and wrinkled her nose. "Of course I still make gingerbread for my customers and it sells very well. Anyway, I know you and I are in agreement over chocolate, but it's the other ingredients I might toss into the recipe that you, personally, might not care for."

He was a realist, and didn't expect to love everything she made. "Which means regardless of whether or not *I* like a certain dessert you make, there's no way to appeal to every single one of my customers.''

She nodded in agreement. ''Very true.''

''That's why we're going for variety, and I'm coming into this taste test with a very open mind.''

Her smile chased away most of the concern etching her features. ''Good. That said, this is my first offering. A Chocolate Mint Truffle Cake.'' She gestured to the elegant-looking cake on the stainless-steel prep table, edged in a pretty scalloped design and garnished with pale-green mint shavings. ''It's rich in texture, but not overly sweet. And the hint of spearmint will appeal to those who like a fresh, cool taste after eating dinner.''

He breathed deeply of the fragrant, chocolate-mint scent. ''It looks and smells fantastic.''

''Well, the real test is in the taste.'' She moved away to retrieve a knife, plate and fork.

''So, who samples all your new recipes before you offer them to the buying public?'' he asked curiously.

''Mostly, whoever is working during the day will taste whatever I'm making and offer their opinion. And then, of course, there is my sister, who is always happy to sample a new dessert.'' She laughed softly. ''But for the most part I have to rely on my own judgment, since it's my name behind the dessert.'' She set the utensils on the prep table and used the knife to cut a slice of the cake. ''Being surrounded by so many sweets and having to sample most of the recipes is what I've come to consider a hazard of the job.''

Uncertain exactly what she was getting at, or what she found so dangerous about her occupation, he asked, ''How's that?''

She cast him a quick, incredulous glance, as if she couldn't quite believe he'd missed the gist of her comment. ''Sampling all these sweets plays hell on a woman's figure. Or at least mine, as you can see.''

Her tone might have held a joking lilt, but the defensive light in the depth of her eyes told another story altogether. She obviously had issues with her shape, though for the life of him he couldn't imagine why. Then he remembered Gretta's well-aimed barbs that had undoubtedly made Kayla think he preferred reed-thin women.

He couldn't change what had happened at the Commerce dinner, but he could let her know right up front his opinion of her figure. ''What I see,'' he said meaningfully as he let his gaze drift leisurely down the length of her body, visually touching her in intimate places, ''is a woman with real curves in all the right places.''

''Thank you,'' she said, still skeptical, though considering the way her nipples were pressing against her T-shirt, she must have enjoyed his lazy perusal. ''You're kind to say so.''

She still didn't believe him. Or was it that she didn't

believe in herself when it came to her own appeal to the opposite sex? It didn't matter, since Jack planned to prove how attracted he was to her, just as soon as the right moment presented itself.

Kayla glanced away from Jack's observant gaze, unsure what to make of what had just transpired between them, or why she'd allowed her insecurities about her weight to come into play. She was a successful businesswoman, but it was painfully obvious that some defense mechanisms were easier to subdue than others.

She hadn't been fishing for compliments, just stating the truth about how her desserts affected her figure, yet the way he'd looked at her, his gaze all hot and hungry...she shivered as she realized the prime opportunity that had presented itself.

She'd already decided that Jack was exactly what she was looking for in order to evaluate the effects of her aphrodisiac candies. And witnessing that glimmer of interest in his eyes gave her the boost of fortitude she needed to follow through on her plan to seduce him, in any way she could.

Even if that meant feeding Jack her enhanced confections in order to spur his lust for her.

Undoubtedly, this was the man she wanted to satisfy her sensual yearnings, to give her body the kind of pleasure it craved and to leave her with a whole lot of sexy memories to recall once they went their separate ways. She wanted Jack Tremaine, and she had no illusions that a physical relationship between them would be anything more than a very satisfying fling.

With that plan in mind, she refocused her attention on transferring a piece of the Chocolate Mint Truffle Cake to a plate for Jack. "Here you go." She placed a fork on the dish and pushed it toward him. "Let me know what you think."

He took a big bite, and she worried on her lower lip as he seemed to savor the taste, the texture, but gave her no outward clue if he liked the dessert, or hated it, other than an undefined, "hm," that could have meant either.

She shifted on her sandaled feet, her own anticipation making her restless. She observed his pensive expression and the way his dark brows furrowed in intense concentration, and took note of his calm, controlled body language.

He was completely absorbed in this moment of judgment, which was exactly what she would have expected from a professional like Jack. After all, he had his restaurant's reputation at stake with the desserts he approved.

There was nothing sexual about his response to sampling the cake. This gave her a starting point from which to judge any change in his composure once she coaxed him to eat one of her aphrodisiac candies. It was going to be interesting to see if, and how, her new creations might alter that serious demeanor of his.

He'd eaten half of the cake before finally breaking the silence between them. "Got milk?" he asked, then grinned at her.

His playful reply was so outrageous and unexpected that she burst out laughing. "Yes, I have milk." She went to the refrigerator, poured him a tall glass, and returned.

He drank half the milk in one long gulp, set the glass on the table, then met her expectant gaze. "I think this dessert is a winner."

She clasped her hands in front of her, giddy with excitement and relief. "So you liked it?"

"I thought it was outstanding." His tongue darted out and cleaned off a smudge of chocolate on his bottom lip. "It was smooth and delicious, and I really like the pleasant mint taste it left in my mouth. All in all, very nice."

"I'm thrilled. Does that mean you're ready to approve this one?" He nodded, and she reached for a file folder, opened it, and withdrew an approval form for the dessert, per their agreement. "Then if you'll just sign right here, the recipe is exclusively yours."

Taking the pen she handed to him, he scrawled his signature on the form, and she gave him the carbon copy. He folded the piece of paper and tucked it into his back pocket. "Looks like you're free to move on to the next recipe."

True, but she wasn't ready for him to leave her shop

just yet. "Since you're here, could I get your honest opinion on something?"

He shrugged those broad shoulders of his, seemingly not in any rush to leave, either. "Sure."

After retrieving the container she'd put on a nearby shelf, she opened the lid to reveal the enhanced candies. Kayla couldn't believe she was actually going to go through with this, but how could she not? Jack Tremaine was the model candidate for her experiment, in so many ways. He was sexy, she wanted him, and she was determined to seduce him.

With a little help from her aphrodisiac sweets, of course.

"I'm creating a new line of candies at Pure Indulgence, and I'd like to know what you think of the taste. Here's the first one I've made." She held the container out to him, and he took one of the chocolates.

He examined it for a moment, then popped the entire piece into his mouth. He chewed thoughtfully, taking his time to enjoy the flavor, just as he had the Chocolate Mint Truffle Cake.

She watched him over the course of the next minute or so, waiting for any kind of specific physical reaction. She had no idea how long it might take for the stimulant to take effect on Jack. She'd read on the Web site that everyone's reaction was different, depending on frame of mind, mood, and how one's body chemistry mixed with the additive. Some people had an instantaneous reaction once the product was consumed. With others it took longer to achieve any sign of arousal.

"Mmmm," Jack murmured after a moment, the rumbling sound strumming along her nerve endings as effectively as a caress. "Espresso and caramel. I like it. What is the candy called?"

"Heavenly Kisses."

A slow, purely male smile curved his lips as he considered that, setting off a conflagration of heat in the pit of her belly. "The taste...the name..." His gorgeous blue eyes darkened with desire as he stared at her mouth. "It conjures up all kinds of possibilities, don't you think?"

Oh, yeah, the possibilities were endless. "Try another," she urged breathlessly, amazed by his gradual transformation from businesslike to much more personal, and aroused by the sexual magnetism that radiated off him.

By all appearances, Jack's system reacted fairly quickly to the aphrodisiac.

He picked up another piece, bit off half of it, and chewed. But instead of finishing it off, he lifted the candy to her mouth, tempting her. "Your turn," he said, and gently slipped the chocolate past her parted lips.

Her tongue touched his finger as she accepted his offering, and he groaned deep in his throat. Her heartbeat quickened beneath her breast. He didn't pull his hand back, but instead traced her bottom lip with his warm fingers, then smoothed his thumb beneath her chin. When he tipped up her face, she found herself mesmerized by the erotic heat flaring in his eyes, the lust that was solely for her.

With his free hand, he took the container from her and set it on the table and out of their way. "How about we see if that candy of yours lives up to its name?" he murmured wickedly, then lowered his head and brushed his lips over hers, slow and seductive, imploring her to let him in.

Coaxing her wasn't necessary, not when she ached for his kiss more than her next breath. She wanted this, wanted *him*, and she wasn't about to refuse the inviting opportunity that had presented itself—even if his lust was induced by an aphrodisiac. For her, the candies had nothing to do with her desire for him. It was stunningly real.

Slanting her mouth beneath his for a better fit, she sighed and welcomed the lazy stroke of his tongue against hers that made her breasts swell and her nipples tighten into hard little points. He tasted so good...like espresso and sweet caramel and hot, aroused man. She couldn't get enough of him.

He stepped closer, bringing with him the delicious heat of his body. She felt him tug the clip from her hair, felt the heavy mass fall to her shoulders and caress her shoulders in a wild disarray. He sank his fingers wrist-deep, twined the thick strands around his fist and held her steady for a long, lush kiss that threatened to consume her senses.

A tingling, insatiable hunger unfurled within her, one she recognized all too well. Unable to stop herself from fully indulging in the reality of Jack kissing her so passionately, she placed her hands on his solid chest. He groaned just as those defined muscles of his flexed beneath her palms.

Emboldened by his reaction, she slid her arms around his neck and arched into him until their hips met and the tips of her breasts pressed against his chest. In return, he skimmed his splayed hands down her back, molding her body impossibly closer to his.

He caressed his palms over her bottom, squeezing and kneading her there before grasping her waist. With a strength that astonished her, he lifted her up so she was sitting on the table—all without breaking their deep, devouring kiss.

His hands slid down her thighs to her knees, urging them apart so he could step in between and press up against her with shocking intimacy. There was no mistaking the thick, unyielding erection beneath the fly of his pants.

He was hard, *for her*. So gloriously, magnificently hard that her breath caught in her chest.

Shamelessly, she wrapped her legs around the back

of his thighs to increase the exquisite pressure right at the crux of her sex, and she felt him shudder in response.

Never letting go of her mouth, he worked her shirt up to her waist and slipped his hands beneath the hem. She immediately stiffened, her first instinct to suck in her stomach, but then he feathered his fingers up over her ribs in such a soul-stirring way that she forgot everything but the sexy way he made her feel. His touch was feverish on her cool skin, and when his thumbs grazed the underside of her heavy, aching breasts she thought she'd unravel right then and there.

He teased and tormented her with the brush of his fingers, heightening her desire, but not quite quenching it. She made a mewling sound she didn't recognize as her own. Like a lover completely in sync with his partner's demands, Jack understood her unspoken need. He cupped her breasts in his large palms, found her throbbing nipples through the sheer lace of her bra with his fingers, and scraped his thumbs across the pebbled tips in the most excruciatingly arousing way.

She felt herself growing wet, felt that frenzied, desperate need building right where he was moving against her in a slow, rhythmic parody of sex. The urgency within her crested, and just when she thought she'd topple over the edge of what she knew would be a stunning climax, he pulled his mouth from hers, buried his face against her neck, and stopped the provocative thrust of his hips against her.

He was panting. So was she. Deep, gulping breaths that did nothing to ease the pulsing tension that had settled in her belly, and lower.

Lord, she'd never, ever, been driven to the brink so quickly—and certainly not with so much clothing in the way—and she instinctively knew it had everything to do with the incredible man who'd kissed her with such fiery possession, and not the half bite of candy he'd fed to her.

"You are so warm, so soft all over," he murmured against her neck, his breath feathering hot and moist across her skin. He nuzzled his damp lips just below her ear and inhaled deeply. "And you smell so damn good. Like a warm cupcake just out of the oven, and it makes me want to take a big bite out of you."

Goose bumps rose on her flesh, and she threaded her fingers through his thick, soft hair to keep him right where he was. "Go ahead," she whispered, a dare that shocked even herself since she'd never been so brazen before.

He gently sank his teeth into the sensitive curve of her neck, then soothed the love bite with the lap of his soft tongue. She shuddered, wanting to nibble on him in return.

Too soon, he lifted his head and met her gaze, looking dazed by what had just happened between them.

He eased his hands out of her shirt and she immediately mourned the loss of his warm touch.

"I'm sorry," he murmured, and shook his head as if to clear it. "I don't know what came over me, except I just *had* to kiss you. I didn't mean for things to get so out of control—"

She pressed her fingers over his lips to stop his words. Even if he didn't understand his reasons for being so amorous, she did, and she refused to let him spoil the moment for her with an apology. "I liked kissing you."

Grasping her wrist, he pulled her hand away from his mouth and flattened her palm on his chest, right over his rapidly beating heart. "I liked kissing you, too. A whole lot."

She nearly melted right there on the spot.

He smiled, his gaze on her face as soft and arresting as a caress. "I think those candies more than live up to their name. Let's hope they don't cause this kind of reaction in everyone who eats them."

Amusement laced his tone, but he was closer to the truth than he realized.

"Would that be such a bad thing?" she asked.

"I suppose not." Placing his hands at her waist, he pulled her off the table, letting the length of her body drag slowly, sensually, against his until her sandaled feet touched the floor again.

She tugged her shirt back into place self-consciously,

even as another surge of awareness sparked between them like wildfire. She wondered what would happen if she coaxed Jack to eat the rest of the Heavenly Kisses—wondered if the aphrodisiac might have the same effect as a dose of Viagra and keep him "up" the rest of the night.

The sinful thought made her entire body shudder with a surge of renewed lust.

He glided his fingers along her jaw and cupped her cheek in his warm palm, his touch infinitely tender. "I think I'd better go, because if I stay I'm gonna eat you up, lick by lick, nibble by nibble, bite by bite...."

A shiver rippled down her spine as his deep voice trailed off, and it was all she could do to swallow the selfish demand, *stay, stay, stay!*

Clearly, the man was thrown off balance by his reaction to her—not in a bad way if the heated glow of possession in his eyes was any indication. Still, he obviously needed time to recover, and she only hoped that as the aphrodisiac faded away and reality settled back in he didn't come to regret what had happened between them tonight.

His first apology had been issued out of shock, which she understood considering he was under a love spell of sorts. A second one, made after careful, clear-headed thought, would be too painful to bear.

No matter how foolish to her heart, a part of her wanted his desire to be authentic and real, and she didn't want anything to shatter that illusion—at least not yet. Not until she'd finished his account and her time with him was over.

But until then, she wanted to live the fantasy. And that meant letting him go before the stimulant wore off. "I'll walk you out front."

He followed her back to the door, which she unlocked for him, but before she could open it, he stopped her with a hand over hers.

"When can I see you again?" he asked.

Her body came alive once again at his question, until she realized that he probably wanted to make another appointment for the next dessert—not go on a date with her.

She considered her next recipe, and how long it might take her to have it ready for him to sample. "How about Wednesday evening?"

"Here?"

A reckless idea popped into her mind, one that was impetuous on her part, and would expose them to a wealth of tempting possibilities, if he agreed. "Actually, the shop doesn't close until nine during the week, which is kind of late. Do you have any qualms about coming to my place instead?"

"Not at all." The idea seemed to please him. "Do you have any qualms about me bringing dinner and a bottle of wine?"

"Sounds wonderful." Walking back to the counter,

she took one of the business cards in the holder and jot-
ted down her street address and home phone number.
Then she handed him the card. "How about seven
o'clock?"

"Perfect."

He tucked the information away. Then without
warning he threaded his fingers through her hair, cra-
dled the back of her head in his big, warm palm, and
brought her mouth to his for another kiss—this one a
blissfully slow, sweet glide of lips and tongue that
made her knees weak and her toes curl.

He managed to end the kiss and pull back before
things spun out of control again, and she was grateful
that he had the willpower to do so, because she certainly did not.

"I'll see you then," he said, and let himself out the
door.

She watched him stroll away and disappear into the
darkened walkways between the shops. "See you
then," she whispered, and touched her fingers to her
still damp, kiss-swollen lips.

AT HOME a half hour later, Jack stepped into the
shower, letting the hard spray hit his tense body.
Hopefully, the cool water on his heated skin would finally ease the fierce erection he'd been sporting since
leaving Kayla's shop. If not, he was in for a long, restless night.

The evening had gone better than he'd expected, even if she'd initially greeted him with a smidgeon of reserve in those eyes of hers. She'd been all business with him—up until the point when she'd asked him to sample her Heavenly Kisses.

At that moment, things had shifted between them in a way even now he couldn't fully grasp or define. He'd been eating her candy, and she'd been watching him so expectantly. And the next thing he knew he had her up on the table and was feasting on *her*.

He groaned at the illicit memory and dipped his head beneath the nozzle, shivering as the brisk water sluiced down his spine and chest to southern regions that needed it the most.

Oh, yeah, her kisses were heavenly all right. He'd suspected from the first time he'd laid eyes on Kayla that beneath her guarded facade was a sensual creature just waiting to be set free. And boy, had she ever let loose! Never in his wildest dreams could he have anticipated the way she rocked his entire world with her uninhibited response to him.

But her unrestrained participation in their kiss told him more about the woman than even she probably realized. That despite her caution, she couldn't hide her attraction to him.

Tonight, she hadn't even tried. And that was enough of a start for him to let her know that he was interested in more than just her desserts. To let her know he was serious about her. Them. Together.

For years he'd put everything on hold in order to build his business and get ahead in life. The stability and financial security he'd sought as a teenager had finally come to fruition. He had all the nice things he'd ever wanted, and enough money to do as he pleased. Even his mother was happy in her new marriage.

Everything was just as he'd planned, except now that he was prepared to take the time for a serious relationship of his own and see where it all led, Jack was coming to realize that when it came to courting a woman, he wasn't quite sure how to handle the delicate process.

Especially with a woman like Kayla, who seemed to need the kind of TLC he'd never given another woman, because for so long his main focus had always been his restaurant.

He felt inept and out of his element, and too used to women who wanted something from him, which had been easy enough for him to deal with by keeping himself emotionally distanced. But because he'd never really looked past his own wants and needs, he couldn't help but worry on some level that he didn't have what it took to give Kayla what *she* needed.

It was an unnerving thought, but he had to try. And to start with, he'd take things as slow as he needed to with Kayla, gradually learn her secrets and cultivate the kind of relationship that could lead to something special.

He was ready for that. And he was ready for Kayla.

4

"WHAT ARE WE doing here?"

Kayla heard the curious note to her sister's voice, and the confusion, too, as Jillian followed her into the boutique next to the café where they'd just had lunch together. Shopping for clothes or other fashion accessories had never been a high priority for Kayla, and she couldn't blame her sister for questioning her reasons for making the spontaneous detour into the exclusive shop when she normally avoided such places like the plague. Wal-Mart and Target were more her style—casual, no-fuss outfits that were durable, inexpensive, and comfortable to wear to work.

She walked up to a rack of colorful blouses and lifted her shoulder in a nonchalant shrug. "I need a couple of new outfits, and I thought you could help me pick out a few things."

Jillian looked taken aback by that announcement. "I can't believe you're asking *me* for fashion advice."

Kayla took in her sister's very stylish outfit with a wry smile. Jillian looked gorgeous in a designer scoop-neck top in red lace, and a black miniskirt that showcased her skinny waist and head-turning legs. She was decked out in all the right accessories, and her tousled hairstyle and tasteful makeup made her look like she'd just stepped off a fashion show runway. In comparison, Kayla felt drab and frumpy in her jeans and plain, loose top.

She'd decided if she was going to have an affair with Jack Tremaine, which she most definitely planned to, then she wanted to look the part of a woman confident in herself. And that meant expanding her wardrobe beyond T-shirts and jeans.

The sensual lingerie she wore made her feel pretty beneath her clothes, but after spending the past two years rebelling against Doug's ultimatum, she was ready to spruce up her outerwear a bit. Nothing too drastic or over the top—just a few nice outfits to wear when she wasn't at the bakery working. Clothes that would make her feel good about herself, inside and out.

"You're a model, Jillian," Kayla said easily as she moved on to a mannequin wearing a simple but flowing summer dress that appealed to her more conservative side. "So why wouldn't I ask for your advice?"

"Maybe because you never have before?" Jillian said with sisterly sarcasm. "Maybe because every time I've asked you to go shopping with me you act like you'd rather eat slugs instead?"

Kayla laughed at that, knowing it was true. "I'll ad-

mit I don't like to shop for clothes. Not if I can help it."
It was a form of torture she tried to avoid. Trying on
clothes had never been a fun process for her, and usually ended up being an exercise in frustration.

"If that's the case, what's the special occasion today?" Jillian's gaze narrowed in a shrewd way that
told Kayla her sister knew something wasn't quite
right and she was determined to find out the truth.
"Come on, what's going on?"

Kayla bit her bottom lip, feeling a moment's hesitation. This was the first time she and her sister had really had a chance to talk since her evening at Pure Indulgence with Jack two nights ago, and now she
debated how much to reveal to Jillian.

She'd been so bowled over by what had happened
between her and Jack. She also felt torn by the fact that
she was using him as an experiment for her aphrodisiac candies without his knowledge. For two days
she'd wrangled with her conscience, and in the end decided to go for it, anyway. She couldn't give up the
chance to enjoy his attention and the sensual way he
made her feel—even if his lust was due to the effects of
a sexual stimulant.

Jack certainly hadn't minded kissing her, she
thought with a secretive smile, and she'd taken that
knowledge into consideration, as well. His desire for
her had been intense, had seemed real, and it had felt
so liberating to let go of inhibitions and be wanton with

him in return—which was something she'd never been able to do with another man.

And since Jack had been caught up in his own needs for her, not once had she worried about how she looked to him. She'd just reveled in the man and the moment and the glorious sensations he'd evoked.

A dreamy sigh escaped her, and she met her sister's gaze. "It's Jack Tremaine."

Jillian blinked at her, her expression perplexed. "What about him?"

She must have lost her sister somewhere, because she usually wasn't so slow on the uptake. "Well... things got a little heated between us the other night when he came to the bakery to sample the Chocolate Mint Truffle Cake for his restaurant."

"And you didn't call me to tell me this?" Jillian's voice rose an octave in chastising disbelief.

Kayla cringed and cast a surreptitious look around them, grateful to find the salesladies taking care of other customers. "I've been busy at work," she said, and fingered the material of a silk skirt that looked cool and comfortable, yet very feminine. "A couple more catering jobs came in from the Commerce dinner, so things have been a bit hectic."

"That's a poor excuse," Jillian grumbled and her frown deepened. "And I thought you told me that Jack Tremaine has a girlfriend."

"Apparently, not anymore." Which made Jack a free

man, in Kayla's opinion. Free to indulge in an affair if he wished, and free to make out with her if the urge grabbed him, which it most certainly had.

"We kissed," she said, then moved on to a peach embroidered top paired off with a pair of khaki drawstring pants that appealed to her casual nature.

Jillian snapped her open mouth shut and hurried up beside her. "Ohmigod, Kayla! You can't just say something like that and leave me hanging." She leaned in close, lowered her voice, and asked, "Okay, 'fess up. I want details. Was he any good?"

Kayla laughed at her sister's eager interest, willing to share at least that much with her. "Oh, yeah, he was *amazing*." He had a mouth made for pleasure, and the pleasure had been *all* hers.

"I'm *so* jealous," Jillian said with a smile, though there was a wistful quality in her tone. "Are you going to see him again?"

"Wednesday night. At my place," she said, as her gaze was drawn to a vibrant purple blouse. She wondered if she could pull off the bright color and off-the-shoulder style. "He's bringing dinner and I'm supplying the dessert."

Her sister grabbed her arm, demanding Kayla's attention, and it didn't escape her notice that Jillian had suddenly grown very serious.

"Hey," Jillian said softly, her knowing gaze searching her features. "You're not in here to buy new clothes and change your appearance for him, are you?"

Before making the decision to add a bit of variety to her wardrobe, Kayla had thought long and hard about that very same question. She'd also remembered the pact she'd made with her sister about never again compromising their identities for a man. After two years of wearing non-descript clothing that hid her body, she was ready to make a few changes, and she trusted her sister to make sure she didn't make any fashion blunders in the process.

"No, I'm not doing this for Jack Tremaine," she told her sister, and meant it. "I'm doing it for *me*."

"That's a *great* answer," Jillian said, obviously very happy with Kayla's levelheaded thinking. "And in that case, we definitely need to find something to show off that figure of yours."

It was Kayla's turn to frown, and she tamped down the rising panic at the thought of "showing off" a body she wasn't one hundred percent satisfied with. "I'd rather not."

"Why not?"

Kayla sighed, surprised she even had to explain to her sister what she already knew. "You know I don't do clingy or form-fitting."

"You don't have to do either, Kayla." Jillian skimmed through a rack of sleeveless poplin shirts. After pulling out one in a pale pink shade, she held it up to Kayla's chest and examined it with a critical eye. "We're going to accentuate your best assets, not blatantly display what you're not comfortable showing off."

Kayla wasn't so sure, and shook her head. "Jilly, I just want to look…"

"Sexy?" Jillian guessed.

Her sister had so easily supplied the one word Kayla had a difficult time saying aloud, and now that it was out in the open, it would be ridiculous of her to deny the truth. "Okay, I'll admit, I wouldn't mind looking a little sexy."

"I'm going to tell you a trade secret, so listen up," Jillian said in that way of hers that combined sisterly affection and tough love. "Sexy is a mind-set. If you feel sexy and confident, then others are going to see that in the way you carry yourself. You need to walk with your head held high, your shoulders pulled back so those great breasts of yours get the attention they deserve, and with a self-assurance that tells the world you love who you are."

Kayla laughed, but deep inside she took her sister's words to heart. "I promise I'll work on all that mind-set stuff."

"All right then, let's get to work." Jillian rubbed her hands together in anticipation. "You have no idea how long I've been waiting for this day to come."

Kayla could only imagine, and for the next hour and

a half she was swept into a maelstrom of coordinating clothes, shoes, and accessories that her sister picked out for her to try on, and deemed the very height of fashion. They laughed and teased as she tried each outfit, and Kayla couldn't ever remember enjoying a shopping experience more.

"This color and style are so great on you," Jillian said as Kayla tried on a two-piece blouse and skirt set made out of gauzy cotton that her sister insisted would flatter her figure. "What do you think?"

Kayla studied her reflection in the mirror, taking in the pretty periwinkle shade, how the hem of the blouse fell past her hips, and the way the skirt swirled loosely around her legs. She liked the outfit...until her sister slipped a silver chain belt around her waist. The delicate design draped loosely over her hips, but in Kayla's estimation drew too much attention to that too-curvaceous part of her body.

Biting on the inside of her cheek, she smoothed her hands over her hips, trying to make them look smaller, which was impossible, she knew. She met her sister's waiting gaze in the mirror. "Are you sure this belt doesn't make me look fa—"

"Don't you *dare* say that awful *F* word," Jillian interrupted before Kayla could finish, and shook a reprimanding finger at her reflection. "You're perfect just the way you are, and don't let anyone let you think otherwise—not even those two dreadful voices in your head."

Her mother and Doug. They were both no longer a part of her life, but still had the ability to affect her confidence. And it was time she kicked their voices right out of her head.

"You're right," she said and lifted her chin, then straightened her posture, which seemed to transform not only her appearance, but her whole attitude. "We'll take this outfit, too, along with the belt."

Another half hour later and they strolled out of the boutique with a new, updated wardrobe for Kayla, and her heart feeling lighter and more carefree than it had in years. They stowed the packages in the trunk of Jillian's BMW and got into the car. But instead of heading back to Pure Indulgence, Jillian turned the vehicle in the opposite direction.

Curious, Kayla asked, "Where are we going?"

"To see my hairstylist," Jillian said with a flash of her famous smile and a sassy toss of her trendily cut mane. "You can't buy all these new outfits and not get your hair cut and styled to go with them."

Her sister's logic was iffy at best, but Kayla knew there was no arguing with Jillian when she made her mind up to do something. So, she reached into her purse for her cell phone, called the bakery to let her employees know that she'd be a little later than expected, and decided to enjoy the rest of the afternoon being pampered.

JACK GRABBED the two grocery sacks from the back of his Escalade and made his way up to the front porch of Kayla's small, single-story house, located in a quiet neighborhood in Mission Bay. The yard was nicely maintained with vibrant flowers growing in abundance in the brick planters surrounding the home, giving the place a well-loved feel. Hanging from a porch beam was a wind chime, and the light evening breeze caused the brass pieces to create a beautiful, melodious sound that made him smile.

Transferring both bags to his left hand, he rang the doorbell. Less than a minute later Kayla appeared, and he found himself staring at the woman in front of him, startled by her transformed appearance. Gone was the woman who wore loose-fitting clothing and kept her hair swept away from her face in a tidy ponytail, and in her place was a bold, daring female that literally took his breath away.

Unable to help himself, he looked his fill. She was wearing a soft, floral patterned sundress that was far from form-fitting, but grazed her curves in a way that teased and tempted his senses and made him wonder what he'd discover beneath that lightweight material—basic cotton or something more tantalizing? His eyes skimmed along the six little pearl buttons that secured the front of the dress over her full breasts, then continued down to her shapely calves and coral-colored toenails.

Swallowing to ease the dryness that had settled in his throat, he lifted his gaze back up to hers. Her makeup was minimal, but what she did have on emphasized her green eyes, her lush mouth, and pretty features. And then there was her silky blond hair, at least two inches shorter than he remembered and layered in a way that it brushed just below her jawline and accentuated the lovely shape of her face.

He couldn't deny that he liked what he saw—mainly because she glowed with a new, subtle radiance that only enhanced the sensuality that was such a natural part of who she was. She looked sexy as hell, and it was all he could do to keep himself from dragging her off to the nearest bedroom, strip her naked, and finish what they'd started at her shop three nights ago.

His body was certainly up for the occasion, he thought wryly, but he wasn't about to rush something so important to their developing relationship—not until he was absolutely certain she was ready to take that next step with him.

Reining in his randy hormones, he masked his need for her with a lazy grin. "Excuse me, I think I'm at the wrong house," he said in a playful tone. "I'm looking for Kayla Thomas."

She blushed at his attempt at humor, and opened the

door wider for him to enter. "Come on in, Mr. Funny Guy."

He stepped into the small foyer, stopped in front of her, and waited for her to meet his gaze. "You look great, by the way."

"Thanks," she murmured, and smoothed a hand down the skirt of her dress in a self-conscious gesture.

The color in her cheeks deepened, giving him the distinct impression that she wasn't used to being on the receiving end of compliments or flattery—and she certainly deserved both.

He lifted his hand and sifted the short strands of her hair through his fingers. His thumb brushed along her neck, and he felt her shiver in response. "And your hair...I like it."

She shrugged in a dismissive manner, as if the new style was no big deal. "It was long overdue for a cut."

He let his hand fall away, and found himself reading beneath the surface of Kayla's actions. He was beginning to understand those insecurities he'd glimpsed a time or two, and he was fairly certain that she was making excuses for her changes because she didn't want him to think they had anything to do with him. And he respected that, along with that strong, independent streak he'd seen flash through her eyes.

He followed her through a living room decorated in oak and earthy tones of peach and beige, and into a cheery, spacious kitchen accented in violet and pale yellow hues.

"Nice place," he said as he set the grocery bags on the large wooden block in the center of the kitchen and started unloading the items he'd bought to make them dinner. "Have you lived here long?"

"About two years." She retrieved two crystal glasses from the cupboard for the wine he'd promised to bring, and set them on the counter. "It's small—perfect for me. Except for the kitchen, which I had remodeled to make it bigger. That way, I can bake at home if I need to."

Everything about her place was cozy, warm, and inviting—a genuine reflection of the woman herself. It made him think of his own custom-built house, so big and open, and too quiet and lonely, he'd noticed lately.

He felt something rub up against his ankle and glanced down to find an orange tabby cat making herself known. Gold-green eyes met his, and she meowed a greeting.

"That's Pumpkin," Kayla told him. "Are you okay with cats?"

"I love cats." And this one was especially friendly. He bent down and scratched her beneath her chin. The feline purred happily. "I'd probably have a cat or dog of my own if I was home more often. Considering how much time I've spent at my restaurant over the past six years, they wouldn't get the attention they need."

"The nice thing about cats is that they're very independent and don't demand a whole lot of attention." She placed a crystal platter on the center island, and beneath the glass dome was an elegantly decorated cake. "And when they want to be loved they'll let you know."

Beside the cake platter, she set out another glass dish with chocolate candies in the shape of small lips that intrigued him. "Do we get to eat dessert first?" he asked, reminding her of the motto she'd shared with him the first night they'd met.

She laughed and shook her head, causing her newly sheared hair to caress along her jaw. "No, I'm going to make you wait and increase the anticipation."

He liked the flirtatious twinkle in her eyes, and the double entendre in her words. "Do I at least get to know what it is? You know, to help build toward the big climax?"

"Ohh, you're good," she murmured, praising him for his play on words. Then she lifted the glass dome off the cake. "This is the next dessert for your restaurant, a white chocolate lace cake layered with raspberry filling and white chocolate buttercream."

"It looks and sounds scrumptious." His gaze lowered to her mouth, which he was dying to taste again, and he thought about those candies he'd just seen. "And what about those sweet lips of yours?" he asked, another sexy entendre that seemed to make the temperature rise in the room.

She smiled. "The lips are part of my new line of candies," she said as one of her fingers traced the edge of the dish. "These are filled with lemon cream and I'm calling them Love Bites."

He groaned. After sampling her Heavenly Kisses the other night, he could only imagine how delicious her Love Bites would taste. Inhaling a deep breath to keep the heat of arousal at bay for the time being, he popped the cork on the bottle of wine and poured them each a generous portion.

He handed her a glass, they touched their rims in a silent toast, then took a drink of the smooth Reisling.

"So, what can I do to help?" Kayla asked, and licked away a glistening drop of wine from her bottom lip.

Jack glanced away from temptation and motioned to the fresh vegetables he'd bought at the market. "Would you mind preparing the salad while I make the main dish?"

"Fair enough," she said with a nod.

She grabbed a knife to cut up the vegetables, and he put a pot of water on the burner to boil for the pasta. Then he tucked a hand towel into the waistband of his jeans as a makeshift apron and began sauteeing the shrimp in a garlic herb sauce. Every so often Kayla glanced up from her own task to watch him as he worked.

"You like to cook?" she asked after a long silent moment had passed between them.

"Sure, I enjoy it, but I have to admit that I wasn't always so great in the kitchen."

"No?" The surprise in her voice was evident. "I would have thought with you owning your own restaurant that being a good cook would come with the territory."

"Not in my case." He'd never intended to be a restaurateur, but had fallen into the business because he'd been at the right place at the right time. A lucky break he'd be forever grateful for. "Let's put it this way. I grew up eating a whole lot of prepackaged foods because it was quick and easy for my mother who was working two jobs to make ends meet. So I never really got the hang of making a meal from scratch. When I opened Tremaine's Downtown and hired my current chef, he taught me a thing or two about cooking that's come in handy."

"Ahh," she said in understanding, and took another sip of her wine.

"And what about you? How did you learn to make all these fancy desserts?" He watched her toss chopped Roma tomatoes into the salad as he stirred the vermicelli. "Did you go to some kind of pastry school?"

"No. I went to college and got a degree in business. My grandmother is the one who's responsible for teaching me how to bake." She glanced over her shoulder at him with a fond smile that reached her eyes. "I spent my summers with her."

"An only child?" he guessed.

"Actually, no." Another drink of wine passed her lips. "I have a sister who is two years younger than me."

"Is she in the baking business, too?"

She hesitated for a brief moment, then said, "She's a cover model. Or was, anyway, until she retired this past year."

"A model?" He couldn't have been any more surprised, or intrigued.

"Do you get *Sports Illustrated?* She was on the cover of the swimsuit issue two years ago." Kayla washed her hands and dried them on a paper towel. "Her name is Jillian Thomas."

He turned the heat off the sauteed shrimp, certain he must have seen her sister's face before if she was a cover model, but he wasn't up on the fashion world enough to recall a specific name. "I can't say her name rings a bell."

"Maybe her face will." She walked over to the refrigerator and pulled a picture from beneath a magnet, then showed it to him. "This is her at a photo shoot for *Cosmo* magazine just before she decided to retire."

Her sister was stunningly beautiful, and dressed in a trendy outfit that drew the viewer's attention to her best assets—her breasts, slim hips, and endlessly long legs that ended in spiked heels. She must have been facing a fan, because her curled hair was blowing around her head in a sexily tousled way, and her come-hither eyes beckoned to the viewer to come and join her for a good time.

He felt Kayla's gaze on him, as if she were waiting for some kind of reaction to her gorgeous sister. A few of the complex pieces of the puzzle that was Kayla clicked into place, making him realize where a few of her insecurities might have stemmed from.

"Hmmm," he said mildly, his gaze on her face. "I can't say that I recognize her, though I can definitely see the resemblance between the two of you. The blond hair, the green eyes, and you both have the same amazing smile."

She glanced from him, to the picture, then back at him again, her brows furrowed into a small little frown of disbelief.

"But back to you, your summers with your grandmother, and how you got into the baking business," he said, dismissing the photograph in favor of conversation with Kayla.

She returned the picture of her sister, then reached into the cupboards for dinner plates. "My parents divorced when I was eight, and every summer my mother would send me off to Arizona to live with my father for three months. Since he had to work, I'd spend my days with my grandmother at her place, which I loved, since she spoiled me rotten."

"How come your sister didn't go with you?"

"She wanted to, badly, but my mother had a slew of pageants and auditions lined up for Jillian, and she never had the extra time to come and visit."

So, Kayla had been shipped off like an unwanted child by her mother. The thought burned in his stomach like acid. "Did your sister *want* to do all those pageants and auditions?"

"No. Not really." She set the table with flatware and laid out potholders for the main dishes. "Our mother was the one who was obsessed with Jillian becoming a model, and since that's all my sister knew, she ended up signing with a modeling agency before she was eighteen."

He transferred the pasta and herbed shrimp to a serving dish, and tossed a little feta cheese on top to give it an extra bit of flavor. "Sounds like Jillian missed out on a normal childhood, and all those summers with your grandmother."

"I definitely consider myself the lucky one."

She smiled, but it was obvious to him that her mother's rejection had hurt, and possibly even affected her still.

"My grandmother and I would bake scones and pies and cakes and cookies...." Her smile grew as she shared her happy memories. "I always came home having gained at least ten pounds, which my mother would disapprove of, and immediately put me on a diet."

Suddenly, Kayla grew quiet, as if she'd revealed more than she'd meant to. He instinctively knew there was much more to that story, but he wasn't about to force her to dredge up painful recollections she wasn't willing to share on her own.

Together, they put everything on the table, then sat down and filled their plates with the fragrant entrée. The salad was tossed with a vinaigrette dressing, and he'd brought a warm, fresh loaf of French bread to go with the meal.

"What about you, Jack?" Kayla asked as she twirled long grains of vermicelli around the tines of her fork. "Do you have any siblings?"

"Nope, I'm an only child." He refilled her empty glass of wine, and topped his off, too. "My father passed away when I was five."

"I'm sorry," she said, her gaze soft with compassion.

He broke off a slice of bread and slathered it with butter. "I definitely miss him and often wonder what it would have been like if he hadn't died, but I had a great mother who did her best to take care of me, and despite some hardships, I never doubted that I was loved." Their life hadn't been easy, which made him appreciate what he had now all the more. "She's happily remarried and lives in San Francisco with her new husband. The closest I've got to a brother is my best friend, Rich. We grew up together in the same apartment building, and now he's the manager of my restaurant."

"That's so great." She smiled and took a bite of her shrimp.

They finished eating their dinner with Jack regaling her with amusing tales and antics about how wild he and Rich had been during their early teenage years. By the end of the meal, she was laughing and relaxed, from the two and a half glasses of wine she'd consumed over the past hour, and from their casual conversation, which was exactly what Jack had wanted.

They both worked to clear the table, and while Kayla washed the dishes, Jack dried the pots and pans for her and put them away. Then she urged him to sit back down, and she set the cake platter and dish of candies on the table in front of him.

She went back to the cupboard for a clean plate, and he filched one of the Love Bites to sample. He put the whole thing into his mouth and chewed, surprised by the smooth, creamy lemon filling that was more sweet than tart.

"Ready for your dessert?" she asked, just as she turned around, dish in hand, and caught him biting into his second piece of candy. She came to an abrupt stop, and looked momentarily startled.

He swallowed and grinned impishly. "I kinda al-

ready helped myself. These Love Bites are fantastic."
He finished off his second piece and reached for a
third.

"I'm, um, glad you like them." She came back up to
the table, her gaze watching him attentively.

For what, he had no idea. Unless he'd been too pre-
sumptuous in sampling the candies. "I'm sorry, was I
not supposed to eat them yet?"

"No...no, that's okay." Her smile reappeared. "In
fact, I'll have one, too."

She tossed a Love Bite into her mouth and chewed.
Yet despite enjoying a candy of her own, she seemed to
watch him out of the corner of her eye as she cut a generous portion of the dessert and put it on a plate.

The slice of cake broke apart, and she grimaced in
obvious disappointment. "Damn," she muttered.
"This cake might be too moist, but I'll re-adjust the recipe if you like the taste." A worried look creased her
brows. "Looks like this particular piece will be a bit
messy with the raspberry filling. I hope you don't
mind."

Oh, he didn't mind one iota. Especially when she'd
just presented him with a prime opportunity to increase the intimacy between them—which he had a
sudden driving urge to do.

He examined the cake thoughtfully. "I have to agree.
It does look a bit messy." He transferred his gaze to her
face and let a slow, sexy grin ease up the corner of his

mouth. "I'm thinking maybe you ought to feed it to me," he suggested. "Remember the problem I had with the Pink Squirrel sauce?"

She laughed, obviously realizing where he was heading with this whole scenario. And with that silent acknowledgement, something about her whole demeanor changed...turned sultry and seductive and oh-so-confident. "I remember."

"Good." Certain they were both thinking the same thing, he grasped her wrist and tugged her gently toward him. "Then what do you say you come here, sit on my lap, and feed me my dessert?"

5

MUCH TO JACK'S PLEASURE, Kayla came to him willingly, without an ounce of resistance, and settled her bottom on his hard, muscular thighs. The thin material of her dress didn't provide much of a barrier against the thickened shaft already straining against the fly of his jeans. And judging by the spark of desire he saw in her green eyes, she was well aware of his erection—and all it suggested. She turned him on and he wanted her.

"I'm ready for my first bite," he encouraged huskily. She lifted her hand toward the cake, then frowned. "I forgot a fork."

Before she could move off his lap and spoil the seductive moment, he settled a hand on her waist and held her in place. "Who says you need one? Your fingers will do just fine."

"All right," she agreed with a smile that was as naughty as it was nice. After scooping up a small portion of the cake with her fingers, she lifted it to his mouth.

His lips parted, and she pushed the confection onto

his tongue for him to taste. God, she made the most amazing, decadent desserts—this one a perfect combination of raspberry glaze and smooth white chocolate buttercream that made him moan in appreciation.

Her eyes were bright with expectation, her breathing deeper than normal, causing her breasts to rise and fall enticingly. "What do you think?"

"I'm not sure," he teased, just because he wanted her to feed him again. And because he enjoyed the touch of her cool, soft fingers against his lips. "I think I need to try another bite just to be certain."

She lifted a brow, obviously seeing past his ploy, but said nothing as she broke off another piece of the moist cake and slipped it into his mouth.

He swallowed, caught her hand before she could pull it away, and met her darkening gaze. Awareness swirled between them, an exciting, shimmering vibration that heightened the throbbing heat settling low and deep in his belly.

"Umm, looks like I missed some...right here." He slowly licked the pad of her finger, then nibbled on the tip, and she squirmed restlessly on his lap. "And a spot right here..." He slid his tongue between her index finger and thumb to clean up a wayward morsel, then scraped his teeth along her palm.

She shivered and gasped, but he wasn't done tantalizing her yet. No, he'd only just begun—and he'd take this seduction as far as she was willing to go.

Dabbing his finger into the frosting and raspberry filling, he touched the sweet mixture to her bottom lip, prompting her to open for him. "Your turn to taste."

Her lashes fell to half-mast, an irresistible smile on her lips as she brazenly took his finger into her mouth, deeper than he'd expected, and used the swirl of her tongue and a light suction to eat off the dessert.

He closed his eyes on a shudder, feeling that erotic pull all the way down to his groin. He dipped his head closer to hers, and skimmed his lips along her cheek. "I *have* to taste *you* now," he said, and heard the aching need in his voice.

She released his finger, and turned her head so that her mouth was right below his. *"Yes,"* she whispered, the one word filled with intense longing.

She slid her palm against his jaw as their lips met in a slow, nuzzling kiss at first, an unhurried exploration that quickly grew deeper, wetter, until having his mouth on hers wasn't nearly enough.

Lowering his hand to the front of her dress, he then popped the first button free, making his intentions known, but deliberately hesitating a few seconds to give her the chance to stop his advance if she wasn't ready to take this next step with him. When she didn't issue a protest, he slowly unfastened another one...and another one, until the material finally gaped open.

He was dying to look at her and see what he'd un-covered. But for the moment he was content to continue kissing her while brushing his fingers over the generous swells of her breasts above the lace edge of her bra.

She made a soft purring sound in the back of her throat, and he took that as permission to proceed. Keeping his mouth fastened to hers, he pushed her bra straps and sleeves off her shoulders, until the fabric caught in the crook of her arms. Then he slipped his hand into the sheer, stretchy material of her bra and eased it down, freeing a full, taut breast before repeating the process with the other side.

Then, and only then, did he end the kiss and take his first look at what he'd revealed. His stomach muscles clenched at the sight of her bared breasts, so plump and creamy, with rosy nipples puckered tight and begging for attention.

"God, you are so beautiful," he whispered reverently, and heard her sigh at the compliment, which made him smile. Swiping a finger into the buttercream frosting, he smeared it around her areolas and crowned the tips of her breasts with a dollop before licking the last of the sticky sweetness from his own finger.

Satisfied with his handiwork, he glanced up at Kayla's flushed face and grinned with lascivious purpose. "Now *you* look good enough to eat."

"Go ahead," she dared in a low, breathless voice.

Curving a hand around a breast, he lifted the soft

flesh to his mouth and used his tongue to remove the mess he'd made. He lapped over and around her hard nipple—slowly, thoroughly, before tugging on the hard peaks with his lips and teeth.

She whimpered and fisted her fingers in his hair. Her back arched to get closer, and he opened wider, taking as much of her as he could into his mouth so he could suckle her hard and strong.

"*Jack*," she implored huskily.

He released her nipple and rubbed his jaw along the plump curve of her breast. "God, I can't get enough of you," he growled, and ran his tongue over her nipple again.

"I know," she panted. "Me, too."

"I have to feel you against me." Tugging his shirt from the waistband of his jeans, he yanked it over his head and tossed the wadded-up material aside. Then he splayed a hand over the center of her back, pulling her close so that her lush breasts crushed against his hot, hard chest.

Their mutual groans of pleasure echoed in the kitchen, and she brought his mouth back up to hers to engage him in another long, deep, tongue-tangling kiss that only seemed to make her more restless, more needy.

Desperate to touch her intimately, to make her come apart for him, he pulled the skirt of her dress to her knees and slid his hand beneath the hem. She sucked in a quick breath, but let him traverse his way up her soft, smooth leg and gently ease her thighs apart, until his fingers touched the damp barrier of her panties.

She moaned against his lips, the sweet, uninhibited sound telling him that she was all his, to do with as he pleased. Without further hesitation, he eased his hand beneath the elastic band of her panties and grazed his thumb along her warm, wet folds, before sinking one finger, then two, deep inside her slick heat.

She gasped and bucked against his hand, her body tightening around his seeking, gliding fingers in a way that told him she was close to climaxing. And because she was so primed and ready, that's exactly where he took her. With sure, skillful strokes of his thumb right where she needed it the most, with his mouth consuming hers, he pushed her up that peak, higher and higher, until she finally took a free-fall into a long, gripping orgasm that left her body trembling and her thighs quivering against his hand.

When it was over, she buried her face against his neck and glided her fingers along his muscled torso, her hands inflaming a carnal hunger within him. Instead of her release exhausting her, it seemed to give her renewed sexual energy that amazed him.

She plucked at his nipples and whispered shamelessly in his ear, "I want *more.*"

More of what, he wasn't sure. More orgasms? It would be his pleasure. But he was just a man, and he'd nearly reached the limit of his control. He was damned close to splitting the crotch of his jeans, and he didn't think he could watch her come again without going over the edge himself.

Framing her face in his hands, he pulled her away, just enough to look into her wild, glazed eyes. "I want inside you, Kayla," he said, his voice rough around the edges. "If you don't want that too, tell me now while I can still think straight enough to stop."

Awe and feminine wonder replaced the heat in her gaze. "You want me that much?"

How could she doubt his desire when the fiercest, hardest erection of his life was pressing so insistently against her hip. Then he realized that she was referring to the kind of passion that went beyond the physical. He felt that for her, too, and did his best to reassure her.

"Sweetheart, I *ache* for you," he said softly. "You drive me *crazy* with wanting you. I even came prepared to make love to you, because I knew after our last encounter that it was inevitable."

Her eyes widened in startled surprise at his admission.

He exhaled a deep breath. "But if you're not ready to take that next step, I'm willing to wait until you are," he said, leaving the decision completely up to her.

"I'm ready," she said, excitement infusing her voice.

Thank God. He urged her to stand up, and he straightened, too. She looked at him in bewilderment, and he explained what he had in mind. "Let's go to your bed." Where he could strip her bare, take his time, and worship every inch of her.

"No." She shook her head, appearing slightly panicked. "Right here. *Now.*"

And then she was all over him, not giving him a chance to argue as she unfastened the button to his pants, then lowered the zipper over his burgeoning shaft. She fitted her mouth to his, kissing him wantonly as she slipped her cool hands inside his briefs and wrapped her fingers around him, then squeezed and stroked his throbbing length until he feared he'd come without the pleasure of being sheathed deep inside her body.

He pulled her hands away before he lost it and managed to utter the word, "Condom."

She stepped back and worked off her panties while he shoved his jeans off his hips and quickly retrieved the foil packet he'd put into his wallet earlier. In record time, he had the protection rolled on, but every good intention he had of taking this first time with Kayla slow and easy went to hell in a handbasket when she pushed him back into the chair, then hiked up the skirt of her dress and straddled his lap.

She moved over him and down his shaft, her breath catching provocatively as he stretched and filled her until she was seated on his thighs and he was buried to the hilt. The connection was so electric that shock waves rushed through him, making his head spin. He'd known the moment he'd seen her that she had a body designed for hot, erotic sex, that her soft, provocative curves would fit him to perfection.

And he'd been right.

She hadn't given him a chance to remove her dress, which covered her hips, stomach, and thighs. And it was then that he understood her purpose, and her reason for not taking this into the bedroom. She wasn't ready to bare her body to him. Despite wanting him, she couldn't shake all her insecurities, even in a moment of passion. As much as he wanted to coax her out of her clothes, he'd let her have her way for now, and lavish attention on what luscious body parts he could.

Threading his fingers through her hair, he tugged her head back, forcing her to arch her spine, which gave him better access to her breasts. Pulling a taut nipple into his mouth, he teased the tip with this tongue and moved his free hand beneath her dress and between her thighs, caressing her slick flesh. She rocked against his hips, riding him with a quick building momentum that urged him to thrust his hips upward in counterpoint, each time driving higher, deeper.

Only when a hot, pulsing climax made her cry out did he let his restraint unravel. His entire body shook with the force of his orgasm, wringing him dry and leaving him wasted.

She collapsed against him and moaned, the soul-deep sound echoing within an empty place in Jack that she was beginning to fill, and he was suddenly overwhelmed by his need for this woman. Beyond the shattering sex they'd just shared, she made him feel... *whole.* And it was a sensation he wasn't willing to give up anytime soon. If ever.

LIFE WAS BETTER than it had been in a very long time. Two days after Kayla's mind-blowing encounter with Jack in her kitchen, she was still walking around Pure Indulgence with a lightness to her step and a dreamy smile on her face. Concentrating on work took effort, since her mind seemed to drift to thoughts of Jack much too often. Especially the way he'd made love to her as if she were the most sensual woman on planet earth.

She sighed in remembrance as she pulled a sheet of cinnamon sugar cookies from the oven, placed them on a cooling rack, then slid another tray in to bake. Jack had most definitely sent her soaring—numerous times—but she had to give credit where it was due. Her Love Bites had no doubt spurred his lust, and her own unfettered passion, and the result had been combustible, spectacular sex.

Unfortunately, she hadn't been able to shed every inhibition with Jack. Sexually, she'd been insatiable, but when he'd suggested they take things into the bedroom she'd been stricken with a sense of dread at the thought of him seeing her completely naked, all her flaws and imperfections on display. Despite the effects of the aphrodisiac candies, some insecurities were harder to break than others, and she was grateful he hadn't pushed the issue.

Humming a cheerful tune, she cut up German chocolate squares and put them on a tray to go in the display case out front. Much to her delight, Jack's amorous behavior had carried beyond their night together. She hadn't seen him in two days because of their busy schedules, but he'd sent her a gorgeous bouquet of roses the day after with a note telling her what a great time he had, and he'd called three times since for no other reason than "just to hear your voice."

She couldn't deny that she enjoyed the attention, but a part of her questioned if his romantic overtures were due to the enhanced candies she'd been feeding him on the sly. She'd experienced enough proof to know that they could stimulate arousal, but she'd begun to wonder if the aphrodisiac could possibly have a lasting effect beyond sating sexual desire.

The possibility made her heart slam hard in her chest, forcing her to admit that her feelings for Jack were subtly changing, that outside of physical attraction he was a man she could fall hard and fast for.

If she allowed herself.

Which she certainly would not.

Jack was a temporary lover, she reminded herself.

And she knew and accepted that once their business deal was over he'd have no reason to be in such close contact with her. No reason to eat her aphrodisiac candies. No reason to lavish her with arousing caresses, drugging kisses. No reason to be the lucky recipient of that magnificent body of his stroking deep within hers.

The thought caused an empty sensation to settle in the pit of her belly. Yes, she'd eventually have to give up Jack Tremaine—because she certainly couldn't feed him an aphrodisiac every day for the rest of his life to keep him as her own—but she still had a few more weeks until she completed his dessert menu and they went their separate ways. She needed to use that time wisely.

Her gaze drifted across the stainless-steel table to the new batch of candies she'd created earlier that day. She bit on her bottom lip, contemplating the sexual power of her candies beyond the arousal Jack experienced after eating one of her sweets. She wondered if her chocolate confections would affect him when they weren't in the same room together, and what the results would be. If he ate her candies without her being present, would he still want her?

She was more curious than anything, because her naughty thoughts went beyond any preliminary testing she needed to do. But she couldn't deny that she found the possibilities of her idea very intriguing. And too tempting for her to resist.

6

"MR. TREMAINE, there's a delivery out front for you. The courier said you need to accept the package personally."

Jack glanced up from the inventory spreadsheet on his computer to the hostess working the lunch shift at Tremaine's Downtown. "Thanks, Tracey. I'll be right there."

He saved the file and closed the computer program, then made his way from his upstairs office down to the hostess stand, curious as to what awaited him, since he hadn't been expecting a personal delivery of any sort.

A young man dressed in a navy-blue courier uniform handed him a small gold box secured with a matching ribbon, and asked him to sign a delivery form. There was no information on the outside of the parcel to indicate who it was from, or what Jack might find inside. Not wanting to open the box with too many employees and lunch patrons watching when he had no idea what to expect, he took the package back up to his office. Sitting in his leather chair, he removed the ribbon and lifted the lid.

The arousing scent of chocolate filled his next breath, and he found a small envelope lying on top of a waxed paper liner with his name written in a feminine script. He smiled, an undeniable rush of anticipation making itself known as he opened the card and read the note inside.

I thought you might like to sample my latest creation. A Chocolate Orgasm. Enjoy. Kayla.

He smiled at the risque name Kayla had chosen for her newest candy, especially since it inspired sinful thoughts of how much pleasure he'd derived from her multiple climaxes a few nights ago. He was bound to enjoy this edible orgasm, too, he was sure.

He removed the paper liner, revealing six chocolates, and his brows rose in what he would have sworn was a figment of his imagination. He picked up one of the treats, and upon closer inspection realized that from one angle the candies looked like the petals of a flower, and from another viewpoint they did, indeed, resemble the curve of a woman's…well, her genitalia.

He chuckled and shook his head, amused by Kayla's new line of candies, and damn curious to find out what this Chocolate Orgasm would taste like.

He took a bite, and out oozed a gooey, white cream center that took him by surprise, but shouldn't have considering the name of the candy and all it implied. He quickly popped the rest of it into his mouth before the thick, sticky filling dribbled down his fingers and made a mess, as always seemed to happen when he sampled Kayla's desserts. He chewed, and moaned at the sweet mixture that combined rich vanilla cream flavored with a hint of almond. It was a simple recipe, but the decadent taste and texture was like ambrosia, and managed to spur all kinds of carnal fantasies in his mind—mainly, of tasting *Kayla's* orgasm on his tongue.

The image of pleasuring her in such an intensely erotic way caused his heart rate to increase and a throbbing pressure to take up residence in his groin. He ate another candy while reliving the other night with Kayla in his mind, and wishing she was here with him now.

It had been two days since he'd seen her, and though they'd talked on the phone, it just didn't compare to being with her in person. He missed seeing her smile and that sparkle in her green eyes. Missed the easy way they teased one another. Missed kissing her and immersing himself in everything honest and pure that made Kayla Thomas such an extraordinarily giving woman.

Absently, he ate another Chocolate Orgasm. Kayla was like an obsession he couldn't shake, an addiction that gave his life new meaning. He wanted more than just her body...good Lord, he was beginning to want inside her heart, too. And if the only way to get there was through hot, hungry sex, then he'd just have to sacrifice himself in the process.

Oh, yeah, like that would be a real hardship. Well, he was hard as steel right now, his entire body hot, his skin too tight—just from thinking about her.

He definitely had it bad, and it felt so, so good.

He shifted in his seat and glanced at his watch. He had an appointment with the City of San Diego to obtain building permits for Tremaine's Uptown in an hour and a half—which left him plenty of time to stop and see Kayla on the way. And if he was lucky, she'd be willing to help him do something about this excruciating condition of his.

KAYLA PICKED UP the office phone on the second ring. "Good afternoon, Pure Indulgence," she recited automatically.

"I'd like to speak to Kayla Thomas, please," came a soft female voice she didn't recognize.

Disappointment dissolved the glimmer of hope Kayla had harbored that it was Jack on the other end of the line. She'd checked with the courier service a half hour ago to verify that her package had been signed and delivered to Jack, but she'd yet to hear from him. Either he hadn't eaten her candies, or her being out of his sight meant out of his mind. And was it really fair of her to send him the aphrodisiac chocolates with such great expectations? No, it really wasn't, she thought on a sigh.

If he'd eaten her candies, the man was probably

walking around with a hard-on to end all hard-ons, wondering what in the hell was wrong with him that he couldn't control his libido.

The thought made a giggle tickle her throat, which she promptly swallowed in favor of greeting the woman on the phone in a professional manner. "This is Kayla. How can I help you?"

"This is Audrey Mann with the Seaside Gallery. We met at the Chamber of Commerce dinner last week."

"Oh, yes, I remember." The woman had raved about the desserts and had taken one of Kayla's business cards. "What can I do for you?"

"I'm hosting an art show for an up-and-coming artist next Friday evening, and I'm expecting at least a hundred guests," Audrey explained. "I wanted to do a dessert table, and I'd like your bakery to cater the job."

"We'd be happy to," Kayla replied enthusiastically, seeing this opportunity as yet another way to gain exposure for her shop. "Would you like to make an appointment to come in and discuss what you'd like, or would you prefer to do it over the phone?"

"Over the phone is fine."

"Great." Kayla pulled out an order form from her desk drawer and grabbed a pen, her mind firmly in business mode. "Tell me what you have in mind and we'll go from there."

Audrey asked for Kayla's opinion on what to serve and the best way to accommodate two hundred people, and Kayla gave the other woman numerous options in different price ranges, depending on Audrey's budget. It seemed the gallery owner wasn't concerned about money, because by the time they'd settled on a menu Audrey had picked the most expensive items and racked up quite a bill.

They'd agreed on a dozen of Kayla's most popular cakes, along with a large assortment of *petits fours* and eclairs filled with a variety of different custards, and a variety of other finger pastries. The cut-up fruit and fondue sauces were added to the order, as well. Audrey had her own employee to serve her guests, which meant all Kayla had to do was supply and deliver the desserts.

"By the way," Audrey said after they'd wrapped up the last of the order. "You're welcome to attend the art show yourself and bring a guest if you'd like."

"Thank you." The woman's invitation made her smile. "That sounds like fun, and I might just do that."

Kayla hung up the phone with an exuberant "*Yes*," just as her office door abruptly opened and Jack walked in, bold as he pleased. It occurred to her that since her employees knew she was working for Jack and he'd been here before, they'd most likely assumed he had an appointment and told him to come on back to her office.

She jumped up from her seat and rounded her desk, glad to see him, yet surprised that he hadn't called first.

Unless he'd wanted to catch her off guard—which was a distinct possibility, judging by the determined set of his features and the blue heat in his eyes.

"Jack! What are you doing here?"

He closed and locked the door, then leaned back against it, looking primitively male, and very sure of himself. "I'm here to extract a bit of revenge for you sending me those candies. You're very naughty, you know that?"

She shivered at the low, rumbling timbre of his voice, her body humming with acute awareness. "You sent me flowers and I sent you candy." She shrugged, striving for nonchalance. "I just thought you might enjoy trying my latest creation."

He lifted a dark brow, obviously questioning her motives. Pushing away from the door, he slowly strolled toward her, an undeniable sexual energy radiating off him. For every step he took forward, she took one back, her pulse accelerating as he neared.

"I'm thinking you sent those Chocolate Orgasms on purpose," he murmured, a soft accusation in his tone.

She didn't confirm or deny his suspicion. Meanwhile, he moved closer and closer, until he had her backed up against the wall next to her metal filing cabinet.

"You wanted me to eat them, and think of you, think of us together like we were the other night." Bracing his hands on either side of her shoulders so she couldn't escape him, he lowered his mouth to her ear. "With me deep inside you and you so tight and warm around my shaft."

A strangled sound caught in her throat, rendering her speechless.

"Well, it worked, sweetheart." His damp lips touched her neck, followed by a warm lap of his tongue that made her tremble all over. "I'm horny as hell, and getting hornier with every passing minute."

His admission thrilled her, and gave even more credence to the idea that her candies truly were an aphrodisiac. He'd eaten them, and hadn't been able to stay away from her.

His hands lowered to her waist, and he ground his hips tight against hers, fitting his erection right at the crux of her thighs. He was long and thick beneath the fly of his khaki pants. Aggressive and demanding.

"You did this to me, Kayla," he rasped against her cheek as his palms slid over her jean-clad bottom and lifted her higher, closer. "You made me hard and aching for relief."

Her head fell back against the wall as her body instinctively arched into his. No, her candies had done that to him. She was just fortunate enough to be the beneficiary of all his pent-up lust.

He increased the pressure against her sex, and the friction of her jeans and the damp silk of her panties against her sensitive flesh touched off a series of spasms deep inside. "What do you plan to do about this problem of mine, Kayla?"

She closed her eyes, caught up in the pleasure simmering just below the surface, beckoning her to let go. "I...um..." She couldn't talk, couldn't think. She just wanted to *feel*. And Jack made her feel exceptionally well.

He lifted a hand, curled his fingers around the nape of her neck, and skimmed his lips along her jaw to the corner of her mouth. "Since this is all your fault, I'm thinking you should put me out of my misery."

He kissed her, a hot, eager melding of lips and tongues that quickly flared into a blazing inferno of need. She wrapped her arms around his neck and his hands found their way beneath her T-shirt to the waistband of her pants. His fingers grazed her stomach before unsnapping the top closure and tugging down her zipper, and there was no doubt in her mind where this embrace was going to lead if she didn't bring him to a halt.

She pulled her mouth from his. "Jack..." She gulped much-needed air into her lungs. "We can't do this. Not here." No matter how much she wanted to.

"Why not?" He was breathing hard, his body vibrating with barely controlled restraint. "The door is locked and I can guarantee that it won't take me long to come once I'm inside you, that's how turned on I am."

If the entire situation wasn't so serious, she would

have laughed. But she was forced to admit that she *was* responsible for his current condition—or at least her candies were—and she reasoned that it wasn't fair of her to leave him in such a painful state of arousal.

His gaze, dark and heavy-lidded with purpose, held hers as he glided his flattened hand past the opening of her jeans and into her panties. "You're wet," he said as his long fingers slid between her cleft and stroked her slowly, languidly, making her body beg for more. "You want me just as much as I want you."

A statement of fact she couldn't argue. "This is insanity," she whispered at the same time that her hips moved of their own volition against his hand, seeking a more illicit caress.

He held her orgasm just out of her reach. "You feel it, too?"

Problem was, she was beginning to feel too much for this man. "Yes." *Oh, God, yes.*

"Then let me in, Kayla," he said, his tone low and desperate.

It was a heartfelt plea she couldn't resist or refuse. She reached for his belt at the same time he sealed his mouth over hers again. She worked his slacks open, took him in her hand, and reveled in the way his big body shuddered just from her touch.

He reached into his pants pocket, withdrew a condom, and hastily sheathed himself. "Turn around and put your hands on the wall to brace yourself," he ordered gruffly.

Caught up in the forbidden excitement of the moment, she did as he asked, and bent forward. He stood behind her, and his hands went to the waistband of her jeans. He tugged them down over her bottom and shoved them to her knees.

She sucked in a stunned breath of air. Too late she realized how vulnerable and exposed this position made her. But before she could bring a halt to this wild tryst, he was smoothing his hands over her bare bottom, opening her for him. She felt the thick head of his penis against her slick heat, and then he was pushing inside of her with a low, unraveling groan. With a driving thrust, he sank to the hilt and her body welcomed him, clutching greedily at his shaft.

He wrapped one hand around her waist, and slipped the other between her legs to bring her to a quick, fever pitch of need that matched his own. The tangle of denim around her knees restricted her, and all she could do was roll her hips sinuously against his as he pumped harder, faster, deeper, in a frenzied rhythm.

She moaned as her climax crested. Threading his fingers in her hair, he turned her head to the side and slanted his mouth across hers. The kiss was erotic and wet—and awkward, but served its purpose to smother her cries, and his own, as they came at the same time.

When the aftershocks finally ebbed, he slumped against her, and they both struggled for breath. Jack nuzzled her cheek, her neck, then finally withdrew from her body at the same time he shimmied her jeans and underwear back up her thighs and hips so she wasn't left buck-naked.

She murmured a self-conscious, "Thank you," considering what she'd just done with him, in the light of day and in her office no less. But, regardless, she appreciated the thoughtful gesture.

He kissed her lips, this time tenderly. "Be right back," he said, and disappeared into the rest room at the rear of her office.

She straightened her clothes, and he returned minutes later looking composed and relaxed. Meanwhile she still felt out of sorts after such a wild sexual encounter. As he approached, she was struck with a sudden surge of modesty that made her face warm to the tips of her ears.

Stopping in front of her, he caressed a finger along her cheek, an amused smile on his lips. "Hey, you're blushing."

A light gust of laughter escaped her. "Well, I have to admit, that was a first for me."

A dark brow arched inquisitively. "Up against the wall sex, or an afternoon quickie?"

"Umm, both, actually."

"It was great. You were great." His low, husky voice

assured her, as did the honest look in his eyes. "Your Chocolate Orgasms are delicious, but nothing compares to the real thing. I needed that, and you, badly."

His sweet words curled around her heart, and for the moment she let herself believe she could provoke such intense passion in this gorgeous, incredible man, and that her candies had nothing to do with it.

"I won't be able to see you tonight because I need to stand in for Rich at the restaurant," he said, his regret palpable. "But how about tomorrow evening?"

Saturday. The weekend. "That's perfect. I'll have another dessert for you to sample, and since the shop closes at six—"

He pressed his warm fingers over her lips, cutting her off. "I want to take you to dinner. Someplace you've never been before."

She liked the sound of that, and she wasn't about to refuse such an offer, not when she enjoyed being with him so much. "Okay."

"Consider it a date then," he said with a concise nod. "I'll pick you up at your place at six-thirty. Bring the dessert, and we'll have it after dinner."

After Jack left her office, she sank back into her chair with a smile, her mind already conjuring up a new aphrodisiac recipe to bring along on their date.

7

SATURDAYS AT Pure Indulgence were always busy, and this one was doubly so due to an outdoor arts-and-crafts show the village was sponsoring. From the moment the bakery opened in the morning, there hadn't been a lull in business. Somehow, in between filling orders and keeping the front displays fully stocked with fresh-baked treats, Kayla managed to prepare a new recipe for Jack to try for his restaurant's dessert menu, as well as create a batch of Caramel Caress candies.

And while she worked, she imagined Jack's response to her newest aphrodisiac candies, and fantasized various erotic ways their night together would end.

The shop closed promptly at six, and Kayla barely made it home in time to take a shower and get ready for dinner with Jack. She jumped into the shower, washed her hair, and shaved her legs. Then she dried her hair until it was silky soft and decided to curl the ends but leave it down, like Jack seemed to prefer it. She applied a light layer of makeup, put on her prettiest lingerie, and dabbed perfume in all the right places.

Minutes later she was dressed in the two-piece peri-winkle skirt and blouse she'd bought from the bou-tique, along with the silver chain belt. She slipped her feet into a pair of cream-colored heels and actually liked what she saw in the mirror—a sexy, confident woman.

By the time Jack arrived at her house at six-thirty sharp she was out of breath from rushing, but miracu-lously ready. The appreciative look in Jack's eyes when he saw her made her feel like a million bucks. She grabbed the cake box with his dessert tucked inside, and off they went to dinner.

It wasn't until they turned onto Harbor Drive and were heading toward the San Diego Harbor that Kayla realized in her rush and excitement that she'd forgot-ten the Caramel Caresses on the kitchen counter at home.

"DAMN."

Jack heard the soft expletive and glanced over at Kayla sitting in the passenger seat of his Escalade. She was staring out the windshield, her brows furrowed in distress. Concern immediately took hold of him.

Reaching across the console, he grasped her hand and gave it a gentle squeeze. "Everything okay?"

She glanced at him, her green eyes troubled. "I for-got the new candies I meant to bring along for you to try."

He didn't understand why that was so important to her, or why she was so upset, but he attempted to bolster her spirits. "You can always send them to me like you did the last batch." He grinned and winked at her.

A seductive smile chased away some of her disappointment as she obviously remembered how that scenario had ended. "You're so bad," she murmured, that adorable blush of hers casting a pink tint to her smooth complexion.

"You seem to bring out that side of me." He brushed his thumb along the pulse point in her wrist, loving the silky texture of her skin. "Any complaints?"

She shook her head, causing the rays of the setting sun to highlight those blond strands with gold streaks. "None at all."

"Good to hear," he replied, satisfied with her answer.

She returned her stare back out the window, taking in the scenery along Harbor Drive, and he replaced his hand back on the steering wheel, though his gaze kept straying back to her profile. She looked beautiful tonight, the soft, purplish color of her outfit complementing her skin tone and adding a radiant glow he was glimpsing more and more of late.

There was a definite change in her since the evening they'd first met. Not just the hair and makeup and clothes, but a more intangible metamorphosis, one that seemed to start on the inside and was gradually working its way out. Self-assurance. Openness. Trust in him. And maybe, the faith to let him in, past those emotional barriers he could still feel between them.

All of those subtle changes made tonight's date all the more important to him. This was his chance to share an important part of himself with Kayla, an opportunity to let her into his life in a way he'd kept private from other women. Tonight was about romance and letting her know that their relationship was about more than just great sex, which seemed to have become a big focal point between them, and very quickly.

Reaching their destination, he pulled into the circular drive that led to the valet parking. He stopped at the curb, and Kayla glanced from the sign in front of the establishment to him, her eyes wide with surprise and pleasure.

"We're at your restaurant," she said, and smiled.

He ran his finger down the slope of her nose, just because he wanted to touch her. "I told you I was going to take you someplace you've never been before."

A young man dressed in a black uniform opened Kayla's door and helped her out of the SUV, while Jack slid out of the driver's side to let his employee take the vehicle to his private parking spot. He retrieved the dessert box from the back seat, met up with Kayla on the sidewalk, and entwined her fingers in his as they walked to the main entrance.

"I've always wanted to come here," she admitted as

she took in the lush plants and tropical garden surrounding them, complete with a small rock waterfall.
"But I never had a reason to come to such a fancy restaurant."

Jack was glad that no one else had ever brought her
to Tremaine's Downtown before. He hoped it would
make the experience more special, for both of them.
"Now you have every reason. Me."

Once inside, they were greeted by the hostess, then
Jack led Kayla to the back of the restaurant and
through the kitchen, where he let his chef know to start
the dinner he had planned. He gave her a quick tour of
the place and introduced her to Rich before leading her
upstairs to a private banquet room with floor-to-ceiling
windows that overlooked the harbor on one side, and
the city skyline on the other.

Kayla stopped at one of the windows, a soft sigh of
awe and contentment escaping her. "The view up here
is absolutely spectacular."

He came up behind her and rested his hands on her
shoulders. "And it's all ours for the night."

She turned around and placed a hand on his chest,
her expression teasing as she plucked at one of the buttons on his dress shirt. "I guess it pays to have a direct
connection to the owner, doesn't it?"

He laughed, and when she would have pulled her
hand away he stopped her, lifted her fingers to his lips,
and kissed the warm, soft tips. "The owner is an easy-

going guy who can be easily swayed by a beautiful woman."

She gave a sassy toss of her hair and added her own witty innuendo to the playful conversation. "Yes, well, I'll try not to take advantage of the owner's generosity."

"For the record, you can take advantage of me anytime you'd like." He leaned in close and lightly touched his lips to hers, which was all he was going to allow for tonight. Sweet, chaste kisses, nothing more.

He strolled over to the table set up for two and withdrew the bottle of champagne chilling in the silver ice bucket. Uncapping the top, he popped the cork and poured them each a glass of the bubbly liquid.

He handed her one of the crystal flutes. "Here's to a memorable evening."

"It already is," she said, and clinked the tip of her glass to his before taking a drink.

Music drifted up from the piano in the bar downstairs, a soft, melodious strain that was perfect for a slow dance. And since they were alone, at least for another ten minutes, he hated to let such a prime opportunity to hold her in his arms go to waste.

He set his champagne on the table then held out his hand for her to take. "Dance with me."

She shifted on her heels, suddenly appearing uncertain. "I'm not very good at dancing."

He wasn't going to let her out of this so easy, not

when it could bring them closer, and not just physically. Sticking with his decision to make tonight romantic and keep sex out of the equation, he wanted to show her just how compatible they were outside the bedroom. And there was a certain element of trust and intimacy inherent in slow dancing. He wanted to experience that with her.

"Says who?" he asked.

"Says me." She took another gulp of her champagne. "I haven't really had much practice at it."

"It's quite easy, actually, and relatively painless," he said with gentle humor as he set her glass on the table next to his, then stepped closer to pull her into his embrace.

He was gratified when she came willingly.

"I hold you in my arms like this," he said, clasping one of her slender hands in his and sliding his other around to rest at the base of her spine. "Now put your other hand around my neck, relax against my body, and let me do all the work. Think you can handle that?"

She looked up into his eyes. "Are you going to give me a choice?" she asked wryly.

He chuckled. "No. Not really."

He moved in time with the slow music and eased her closer, until they were aligned from chest to thighs and she was in sync with his every step. He was surrounded by the warmth and softness of her body and the arousing scent of her perfume, and he couldn't imagine another place he'd rather be at the moment than right here with Kayla.

He dipped his head and gently slid his cheek to hers. ''Nice, huh?''

''Umm, very nice.'' Tentatively, she laid her head on his shoulder and sighed, and her warm breath tickled his neck.

Her actions held nuances of the trust and intimacy he'd hoped for, but he knew this was just the beginning. He lazily stroked his hand up and down her back, wondering when the last time was that someone had just held her and made her feel cherished.

With the way she was snuggled up against him, all lush and warm and soft, it was inevitable that his body get turned on. And because that wasn't his intent tonight, he knew he had to end the embrace now, before that part of his anatomy passed the point of no return.

With a great amount of reluctance he eased to a stop and let her go, just as their waiter arrived with the first and second courses to their meal. They sat down at their table and were served bowls of lobster bisque, along with a platter of hors d'oeuvres that consisted of smoked salmon, paté, lobster medallions and Caspian Sea caviar.

Once the server was gone and they were alone again Kayla took a taste of her soup and moaned blissfully.

Jack spread a dollop of caviar on a cracker and grinned. "I take it you like the bisque."

She nodded her approval. "It's so incredibly smooth and creamy. I think this could become as addictive as my desserts."

"Give the smoked salmon and paté a try," he said, and she helped herself to both, then added a few of the lobster medallions for good measure.

He watched Kayla savor her meal, and decided he liked being with a woman who actually *ate* the food on her plate, instead of pushing it around to make it look like she'd taken a few bites because she was worried about her figure. Fine cuisine was a big part of Jack's life, and it was nice to find a woman who shared that passion.

"This place is so elegant, and the food is outstanding," Kayla complimented as she waved her fork over the bisque and hors d'oeuvres. "You never did say how you got into the restaurant business. Do you mind me asking?"

"Not at all." This was the opening he'd been waiting for, an ideal segue for him to share more intimate details about himself and his past and the man he'd become. "Do you remember what this restaurant was before it became Tremaine's Downtown?"

She thought for a moment on that as she took a drink of her champagne. "That was such a long time ago. I believe it was a casual kind of restaurant, wasn't it?"

"It was six years ago, and back then the place was called Bluebeard's."

Her eyes lit up in recollection. "That's right. Now I remember. It was a bar and grill, wasn't it?"

"Yes," he said, and absently swirled the sparkling liquid in his flute before finishing it off. "When I was seventeen, I was hired on as the dishwasher, and it was the perfect part-time job while I finished school then went to college. Over the years I worked my way up to being a waiter, then a bartender, and finally, the manager of the restaurant."

"Very impressive," she said.

He shrugged off her compliment, because the ambition to make something of himself had driven him hard from a very young age. He'd always been looking ahead at a better raise, that next promotion, and anything else that would take him where he wanted to go—and that place was financial security. The kind he'd grown up without.

"Jimmy was the owner who initially hired me," he said, back to his story. "And when he died a few years later his wife, Molly, took over the restaurant, which was a huge mistake since she didn't have much interest in Bluebeard's at all. She held on to the place because it provided a small extra cash flow for her, but eventually she sucked the restaurant dry financially. One day the employees came in for work and Molly announced that Bluebeard's was on the verge of bankruptcy and she was shutting the place down.''

Kayla winced, obviously understanding the ramifications of that. ''Dare I ask what happened?''

''The story ends happily,'' he assured her.

He paused as their waiter returned to clear off their plates and serve them their main entrée of chateaubriand, a roasted tenderloin of beef accompanied by an array of fresh steamed vegetables topped with béarnaise sauce.

He cut into the beef and found it tender and perfectly prepared. ''Anyway, I saw this as the ideal opportunity to finally open a restaurant of my own, which I was considering anyway. I made an offer on the place, and since it was so run-down and Molly was so anxious to unload the restaurant, we came to a quick, mutually acceptable price and the establishment became mine.

''Unfortunately the place needed a whole lot of work for what I envisioned,'' he went on as he refilled each of their champagne glasses. ''And because I was determined to make a success of my restaurant when it opened, I took out an additional loan for major renovations and shut the place down for six months while I had the establishment redesigned and restructured. The inside was completely gutted then redecorated, and I had this upper level added on, too, for private parties and banquets.''

"That's an amazing story." She dabbed the corners of her mouth with her linen napkin then spread it on her lap again. "And soon you'll be opening your second restaurant. That has to be exciting."

"Exciting and scary," he said, knowing she'd understand since she had a business of her own. "It's like starting all over again."

"After tonight's meal, I'm certain the success of Tremaine's Downtown will carry over to Tremaine's Uptown." Then the corner of her mouth twitched with unmistakable humor and delight. "And of course you'll have your new dessert menu to draw your customers back again and again."

"That I will," he said.

For another half hour they ate their dinner around companionable conversation, until Kayla declared that she was unable to eat another bite.

"Not even the dessert you brought?" he asked, setting his fork on his empty plate.

She leaned back in her chair, looking impish. "Okay, maybe a bite."

He laughed and when the waiter returned to clear their dinner plates he asked the young man to bring back the dessert he'd brought to the restaurant, along with coffee for both of them. Minutes later, their order arrived—fresh coffee and two slices of the cake Kayla had made for him.

This evening there would be no feeding each other,

or asking Kayla to sit on his lap. He knew all too well how fast things could turn wild and hot between them, and there was no sense tempting himself with what he wasn't going to take tonight.

"Tell me about the cake," he prompted, curious to know what it was, and what to expect.

"This is a coconut lemon cake," she told him as she stirred cream into her coffee. "The inside is an extra-moist blend of coconut-flavored cake enhanced with fresh lemon juice and grated peel. The outside is topped with a halo of delicate coconut flakes on a lemon glaze."

He took a few bites to really savor the taste, and like every dessert that had come before, he liked it. The moist cake dissolved in his mouth, and the coconut and lemon flavor was a combination that worked well together and left a pleasant taste in his mouth afterward.

Kayla ignored her own slice of cake and watched him eat his dessert. After a few silent moments had passed, she asked anxiously, "Well?"

He wiped his mouth with his napkin and grinned. "It's great. I'll take it."

She visibly relaxed in her chair. "You're easy to please, you know that?"

"You make it easy on me." He took a drink of his coffee, and forked off another bite of the cake. "You've given me three very unique and diverse desserts, and I think each one will be a hit."

Finally, she started in on her own piece of cake. "I was thinking, maybe you'd like to add a cheesecake to the menu?"

He considered the suggestion, and agreed that cheesecake was a popular item. "What did you have in mind?"

"I came up with a few flavors I'd like to run by you, actually." She licked a smear of lemon glaze off her bottom lip, her expressive green eyes lighting up with exuberance. "There's a Dutch Apple Streusel Cheesecake, Kahlúa Coffee Cheesecake, a Dulce de Leche Caramel Cheesecake, or Chocolate Pecan Turtle."

He chuckled and shook his head. "And you expect me to choose just one?"

"Eventually." She smiled, drawing his gaze back to her sexy mouth and reminding him of the immense pleasure she'd given him with those lips of hers. "How about I make a small example of each flavor, and you can pick the one you like the best? I can have them ready for you to taste by Wednesday afternoon."

"That would be perfect." As she was. Every single curvaceous inch of her.

And that easily, that quickly, his body reacted, growing heavy with a need that made him question his personal promise about not making love to her tonight.

AFTER DESSERT, the drive back to Kayla's house was made in a companionable silence, which gave her too much time to think about how the night might end. She knew how she *wanted* it to end. But despite the awareness and sensuality that had been undeniably apparent between them all night long, there was also a level of reserve on Jack's part that left her feeling off balance and uncertain about herself, and them. Now she really wished she hadn't left those Caramel Caresses sitting on the counter at home.

If she'd brought them along as planned, there wouldn't be any doubt in her mind that they'd end the night in a hot, passionate encounter. Just like every time before that he'd eaten her aphrodisiac candies.

Refusing to let insecurities or those too-distracting voices in her head ruin what had been a great evening, she let her mind drift to more pleasant thoughts...like how at ease and comfortable she felt around Jack. She couldn't ever remember feeling this way with another man before.

Not even Doug.

Especially not Doug.

With Doug there had always been too many expectations on his part that left her constantly worrying about whether or not she measured up. Did she look all right? Had she said or done the wrong thing? And no matter how hard she tried to please him, he'd always find something to criticize.

But with Jack...she was beginning to relax and feel comfortable in her own skin, which was a first. But as much as that realization increased her inner confidence, she was all too aware that she was gradually opening herself up to Jack emotionally, which hadn't been part of her plan. When this affair of theirs ended, she wanted to walk away with her heart intact, and she'd do well to remember that.

He pulled into her driveway, then walked her to her front door. A sudden burst of nervous energy took hold, and butterflies swarmed in her stomach.

"I had a wonderful time tonight," she said as she dug around in her purse for her keys. Finding them, she then glanced back up at Jack's face. The porch light illuminated his strong features and fathomless blue eyes. "Thanks for taking me to your restaurant."

"It was my pleasure." He plucked the keys from her fingers, then unlocked and opened the door for her.

He was being so polite, so chivalrous, and she knew that any advance tonight was going to be up to her.

"Would you like to come in?" she asked before her small allotment of courage fled. "I still have those candies you haven't tried yet." Good God, she hoped she didn't look as desperate as she suddenly felt.

"I'm tempted to take you up on that offer, but I'm going to pass tonight." He feathered his warm fingers along her jaw, the touch more soothing than sexual. "It's late and you look tired."

She gave a jerky nod of understanding, even as a huge swell of disappointment settled over her. She'd known from the moment she'd forgotten her Caramel Caresses at home that they wouldn't make love, but that knowledge, combined with Jack's subtle rejection of her invitation to come inside, didn't make her heart ache any less.

Her all-consuming need for Jack was having less and less to do with her experiment, and everything to do with a deeper yearning she couldn't ignore.

She inhaled a deep, startled breath as her mind tried to grasp the ramifications of those thoughts. Oh, Lord, she was falling for Jack Tremaine, despite her best intentions to keep her emotions out of their relationship. And that realization scared the heck out of her.

Still, she was determined to enjoy their affair, and her short time with Jack. And that meant being daring enough to invite him to join *her* for a night out, without her desserts as a lure.

"I meant to mention this earlier," she said with a tremulous smile. "I'm catering an art show next Friday for the Seaside Gallery, and I was invited as a guest. Would you be interested in coming with me?"

He smiled that sexy smile of his, which made her feel a bit better. "Are you asking *me* out on a date?"

A date. She liked the sound of that. "Yes, I guess I am."

"Then I accept." He brushed a tender kiss on her temple. "Good night, Kayla."

"Good night," she whispered, hating the longing in her voice that she knew he had to have heard.

She went inside the house, stripped out of her clothes, and put on a silky chemise, still disappointed about how the evening had ended, but feeling hopeful about their date next Friday. After washing the makeup from her face and brushing her teeth, she crawled into her big lonely bed with only Pumpkin for company. The feline loved to cuddle, but she was a poor substitute for the warm male body Kayla had been hoping for.

8

"I THINK IT'S going to be a tie between the Dutch Apple Streusel Cheesecake, and the Chocolate Pecan Turtle," Jack announced after sampling the variety of cheesecakes Kayla had set out on the stainless steel table for him to try.

Kayla smiled, the first genuine one in days—ever since Jack had dropped her off at her house and she'd spent an endlessly long night tossing and turning in her bed.

"What do you know, those are my two favorites as well," she said. "How are we going to narrow this down to just one?"

Jack rubbed a finger along his jaw as he contemplated her question. Finally, he met her gaze, his eyes such a brilliant shade of blue her stomach fluttered in keen awareness. The desire she'd been fighting since the moment he'd walked into Pure Indulgence nearly an hour ago expanded, making her ache all over for his touch.

His kiss.

Any kind of physical contact at all.

So far, since he'd arrived he'd been all business, and she was frustrated and confused by his pragmatic demeanor. Then again, maybe he needed a bit of an incentive to be more forward with her. Maybe he needed to eat one of the Caramel Caresses she'd set aside to feed him after they wrapped up this selection process.

That would probably do the trick and end his too-noble behavior. A few candies, and he'd likely ravish her right there on the work table.

The provocative thought made her pulse quicken.

"What do you think?" she prompted, anxious to follow through on her idea. If need be, she'd ravish Jack—that's how badly she craved him.

"I think since they're both so vastly different in taste, I'd like to go with both for my dessert menu."

She hadn't expected that. "Are you sure?"

"Positive." He nodded succinctly.

"Okay." She hooked a finger toward the back room. "I left your paperwork in my office. I'll be right back, and we can sign off on these desserts, too."

"Great." He smiled, and an instant surge of heat sped through her veins.

Good Lord. She *had* to have him again. Here. Tonight. And she would, just as soon as they finished with business and she was able to feed him a few of her Caramel Caresses. She'd rev up his libido, and since her employees were gone for the evening and they were all alone, they'd both enjoy another hot, illicit tryst right there in the back of her bakery.

She went to her office, grabbed the file folder for Tremaine's Downtown, and returned to the kitchen area. Jack was across the way, examining the proof boxes and the industrial-sized dough-and-batter-mixing machines. He seemed fascinated by the equipment— while she found herself just as captivated with the sight he presented.

Whether front or backside, he was a gorgeous hunk of male. And in this case, she had a spectacular view of the way his broad shoulders filled out his blue cotton T-shirt and of the defined muscles that bisected his spine. She took in his narrow waist, his lean hips and a world-class ass that made her envy the denim that hugged his butt in such a loving way.

Her breasts swelled in reaction to her naughty thoughts, her nipples tightened, and she felt tingly all over. She didn't need the benefit of eating her candies to want Jack, and she wished he felt the same.

She swallowed the groan in her throat and instead inhaled a deep breath that did little to calm the desire taking hold. "Here you go," she said, drawing his attention back to the fact that she'd returned. The sooner he signed the exclusivity form, the quicker they could move on to more...pleasurable matters.

He strolled back to the table and read through the paperwork for the two cheesecakes before signing on the bottom line. She gave him a copy of the form, then closed the file folder and pushed it out of the way for now.

"What kind of dessert would you like to consider next?" she asked.

He leaned a hip against the counter and pushed his hands into the front pockets of his jeans. "I know this isn't exclusive, but I've tried the shortbread tarts you carry out in the front display case and I think they'd make a nice addition to the dessert menu. They're rich and buttery, but not overly sweet. Just a smooth cream-filled pastry that we can top off with fresh strawberries or kiwi slices."

"Sure, you could do that." She boxed up the rest of the sample cheesecakes to put into the refrigerator. "The shortbread tarts are one of our most popular items."

"Then let's go with that." He helped her remove the plates and utensils and set them in the sink. "And with the cheesecakes and tarts, I think that wraps up the dessert menu."

She'd known from the moment that Jack had hired her that their relationship, business or otherwise, would inevitably come to an end. But there was no denying the sharp twist of dread Kayla felt in the vicinity of her heart. The one that told her she'd allowed herself to get involved with Jack on a much deeper level than she'd ever intended.

But business was business, and she'd made a commitment to Tremaine's Downtown that superceded any feelings she might have developed for Jack. Making sure she satisfied the terms of their deal was her first priority.

With that in mind, she asked, "When would you like to start receiving the new desserts?"

"I need to have new menus made up and printed, so let's say the beginning of next month?"

That gave her a few weeks to get everything prepared on her end and work his desserts in with her other weekly orders. "That's doable for me."

She returned to the table, which had been cleared of everything but the box of Caramel Caresses that she'd deliberately set out earlier. They might have just finished up their business transaction and no longer had a reason to see one another on a regular basis, but she had tonight with him, and Friday at the art gallery show. And she was feeling shameless enough to take advantage of both opportunities, because she knew that once she had no professional reason to see him anymore, their current relationship would return to a more casual, businesslike exchange.

Reconciling herself to that fact was getting harder and harder to do.

She brought the box of candies forward, lifted the lid, and glanced up at Jack with a hopeful smile. "Since I forgot to bring along my Caramel Caresses to dinner the other night, I was hoping you'd give one a try and let me know what you think."

He leaned close, bringing with him the warm male scent that was uniquely his, and peered at the candies she'd revealed. Then he looked up at her with amusement dancing in his eyes.

"You know, I couldn't help but notice that the last batch of candies you sent to me, the Chocolate Orgasms, resembled a very intimate female body part." His voice had turned into a low, mesmerizing murmur and a sizzling heat was slowly replacing the humor she'd seen in his gaze only moments before. "And now these...am I mistaken, or do they look like the curve of a woman's breast with that small dollop of chocolate right in the center serving as a nipple?"

She watched him graze the tip of those candies with the pad of his finger and felt that touch as surely as if he'd just caressed her own taut nipple.

"You have a very vivid imagination," she said, trying to suppress a visible shiver, and failing miserably.

He lifted a dark brow. "Do I?"

It was a question, a dare for her to admit just how naughty her candies were. "You're not mistaken. It's all part of the new line. I wanted the sexual resemblances to some of the candies to be subtle, but definitely arousing."

"Then you achieved your goal. The candies are very sensual, in name and taste. And erotic." His deep tone was equally so. "Just the name of the candies are enough to turn me on. And when I eat them, they make me think of you, and I'm beginning to learn that that can be a very dangerous thing."

She tipped her head and slanted him a beguiling glance, enjoying the direction of their conversation. "Dangerous, how?"

He gently brushed a stray strand of hair off her cheek before tucking it behind her ear. "Because after eating those candies and thinking of you, then I have to have you."

His touch electrified her, making her skin feel ultra-sensitive. "Sounds like a very *good* thing to me."

A lopsided grin curved his lips, though his dark eyes seemed to eat her up whole. "It's not so good when I'm eating your candies alone."

She felt breathless, anxious, and excruciatingly aroused. "I'm here now, so let's see what you think of these."

Taking one of the Caramel Caresses out of the box, she brought it up to his mouth at the same time she heard a clanking noise from out in the service area of the bakery. Startled, she jerked her gaze toward the swinging door leading to the front counters.

Jack must have heard the same clatter, because he frowned and cocked his head to listen for any other sound. This time, there was no mistaking the jangling of keys and the *click, click, click* of high-heeled shoes on the tiled floor.

"Sounds like someone's here," he said in a low, uneasy tone of voice. "I thought you locked the front door after I came in this evening."

"I did," she said, her heart slamming in her chest at the thought of the place being burglarized.

"Stay put," he ordered, and started around the table, then came to an abrupt stop when her sister appeared in the doorway leading to the kitchen. She was wearing a cute little minidress that molded to her centerfold figure, and holding a peanut crisp bar in her hand that she'd no doubt filched from the case out front.

Her sister, who had a key to the shop, but had never used it before tonight.

How convenient, Kayla thought wryly, and put the piece of candy back in the box for safekeeping.

While she was relieved to see that she hadn't just experienced a break-in, she was frustrated that her sister had put a major crimp in one of her last attempts at seducing Jack. She'd been so, so close to feeding him the candy. So close to enjoying the physical pleasure that always followed.

"Jillian?" she questioned. "What are you doing here?"

Her sister's wide-eyed gaze slid from Jack, to Kayla. She'd taken a bite of the peanut crisp bar before walking into the kitchen, and she quickly swallowed what was in her mouth. "Well, I was on my way back from having dinner with a friend, and I saw your car in the parking lot. I got worried since it's so late. I just wanted to make sure you were okay, to see if you needed help packaging up an order, or anything else."

"I'm fine." She could hardly get upset at Jillian for being so damn sweet and protective, but boy, did her sister's timing suck. "I was just going over the last of the desserts with Jack here."

"Whom I finally get to meet." A dazzling smile lit up Jillian's face as she strolled forward on her four-inch heels with a grace Kayla couldn't have pulled off in a million years. She offered the hand that wasn't sticky from the peanut butter treat. "It's such a pleasure to finally meet you."

"Likewise." Jack shook hands with Jillian, his grin amicable. "The picture Kayla showed me of you doesn't come close to doing you justice in person."

"You're kind to say so." Jillian shifted her gaze back to Kayla and bit on her lower lip. "I'm really sorry, Kayla," her sister said with a small wince of contrition. "I had no idea you had company."

Kayla shook off the last of her annoyance, because her sister's intentions had been nothing but pure. "I appreciate you checking up on me, Jilly. We just finished wrapping up the dessert menu for Tremaine's Downtown."

"How exciting." Jillian turned back to Jack, her stylishly cut hair swirling around her shoulders like a blond cloud. "These new desserts that Kayla has been making for your restaurant have been amazing. What cheesecakes did you decide on?"

"The Dutch Apple Streusel, and the Chocolate Pecan Turtle," Jack replied.

Jillian sighed and pressed a hand to her chest. "Those sound sooo good. I was dying to taste them earlier, but Kayla wouldn't let me have a piece out of the sample cakes until you'd tried them first."

"You'll be happy to know that there's plenty left over," Kayla cut in, knowing that's exactly what her sister was shamelessly angling for. "I'll wrap up a few pieces for you to take home."

Jillian grinned impishly. "One of each, pretty please?"

"Sure." Kayla headed back to the refrigerator, pulled out the boxes of sample cheesecakes, and went about packaging up the dessert for her sister.

She stood across the room, facing Jillian and Jack as she worked, which enabled her to watch them engage in an easy conversation, punctuated by her sister's laughter and a smile or two from Jack.

At the moment, Kayla couldn't help but envy her sister—her great personality that never failed to garner male attention, her fabulous body, and the fact that she could eat five slices of cheesecake in one sitting and not gain an ounce—compliments of the genes Jillian had inherited from their reed-thin mother.

That same mother's words drifted through her mind. She'd compare Kayla to Jillian and constantly ask why Kayla couldn't be more like her sister. She'd ask why Kayla didn't try harder to lose weight when Jillian could maintain her figure just fine. Doug had done the same on occasion, but what neither of them had ever understood or wanted to believe was that she and her sister were built differently. And Jillian had been born with a great metabolism, and Kayla had not.

Kayla's stomach churned, her insecurities flaring hot and bright inside her chest. She expected to see Jack ogle Jillian, just like every man tended to do when she was in a room. She was even prepared to experience that sensation of fading into the background that accompanied her sister's vibrant presence. But Jack merely remained polite and friendly to Jillian, and seemed completely immune to her knockout looks and personality.

Kayla couldn't help but feel a bit of shock over his lack of reaction to her sister.

Finished wrapping up the cheesecake for her sister, Kayla came up beside the two of them and handed Jillian the bakery box with a smile. "This ought to keep you happy until tomorrow morning," she teased.

Jillian wrinkled her nose playfully at Kayla. "Then expect me back in here by tomorrow afternoon for a refill. But, for now, I'm out of here." She gave Kayla a hug, then turned back to Jack. "I'm so glad I got the chance to meet you, and I hope to see you again."

He smiled. "I'm sure you will."

Kayla walked Jillian to the front of the bakery, let her out, and locked the door behind her. Then she returned to the back of the shop where Jack was waiting for her, leaning casually against the counter. The moment with the Caramel Caresses was lost, and she wasn't in the mood to try to recapture the desire she'd been feeling before her sister had arrived. Instead, she cleaned up the small mess she'd made while getting Jillian's dessert boxed up.

"Are you okay?" Jack asked after the silence had stretched much too long between them. "You've been pretty quiet since your sister arrived."

She forced a smile that felt too stiff on her lips. "I'm fine."

The skeptical look on his face told her that he didn't believe that for a second. "Then why do I get the feeling that there's something going on in that head of yours?"

She was startled to think that he might understand her well enough to see beyond the nonchalant facade she'd erected. It was a scary thought, because it had been years since she'd let a man that close. And it had been just as long since she'd trusted another person besides her sister with her emotions.

She gave a casual toss of her head. "It's that vivid imagination of yours."

She was trying to lighten the moment with humor, but he wasn't going for it and remained serious. His gaze was filled with a concern that caused her heart to pound hard in her chest—and made her long to believe in this man who seemed genuinely to care about her feelings.

He moved toward her, closing the distance between them, and grasped her hand in his. "Talk to me, Kayla," he said, his soft voice encouraging her to open up to him.

Still, old habits died hard, and protecting her emotions was instinctive. "I'm sure it's nothing you want to hear."

His thumb rubbed gentle, soothing circles on her palm. "Try me, sweetheart."

Jack was too persistent and her resistance caved. Everything that had been bottled up within her for so long—fears, doubts, and vulnerabilities—worked their way to the surface, aching to be set free.

The night certainly couldn't get any worse, she reasoned, and what did she have to lose anyway? Nothing except Jack, and she knew he would be out of her reach after Friday night anyway.

She exhaled a deep breath, mentally preparing herself for the conversation to come. "As you can see with your own eyes, Jillian and I are as different as night and day."

A small frown furrowed his brows. "No, not really. At least *I* don't think so."

The man wasn't dense, nor was he blind, and she was frustrated at his attempt to placate her. She was referring to more than just their blond hair, their green eyes, and the smile that Jack claimed they both shared. So, she was just going to have to be blunt with the man.

"I'm talking about our body types and our figures," she said, trying to tamp her frustration. "You can't deny that we're opposites."

"And that's an issue because?"

She pulled her hand from his, exasperated at how difficult he was making this for her. "It's always been an issue between us." Or at least others had made it an issue for Kayla, which in turn had affected Jillian, as well.

"How so?" he asked curiously. "The two of you seem close, and I can't imagine that you'd let something like body type differences get in the way of your strong relationship."

No, she and Jillian had been fortunate that the experience and their insecurities had bonded them closer as sisters, instead of pulling them apart. Their sisterly love had survived, despite their mother's demands and skewed visions that had made life difficult for the two of them—in vastly different ways.

The only way Jack would fully understand what she was getting at was for her to start at the very beginning. So that's exactly what she did. "I grew up with a mother who constantly compared me to Jillian, and not in a flattering way, either."

His lips flattened into a thin line of disgust. "I gathered as much from what you told me the night we had dinner at your place."

The man was very astute, because she hadn't directly mentioned the way her mother had treated her.

"For as long as I can remember, my weight and the way I looked was a problem for my mother. I can recall as early as the age of five the difference in the way my mother would treat me and Jillian. Especially out in public. If we were walking through a grocery store or mall, my mother would always hold Jillian's hand and I'd end up behind them a few feet, by myself."

Kayla also remembered the way Jillian would glance over her shoulder during those times, her expression so heartbreakingly sad, because even at that young age she understood the pain their mother's actions had caused Kayla. And neither one of them could do a damn thing about their mother's blatant favoritism.

"People would stop and exclaim about what a beautiful child Jillian was," Kayla went on, not meeting Jack's gaze because she didn't want to see the pity that might be present in his eyes. "And my mother would go on about all the pageants Jillian had won, and never once acknowledged my presence, or the fact that I was her daughter, too. At least not until we were in the car and out of hearing range of other people. Then my mother would give me a lecture about my weight, and how I could get the same kind of attention if I'd just make an effort to take care of myself and watch what I ate.''

She laughed, but the sound lacked humor. ''The funny thing is, food became a source of comfort for me. The more my mother tried to deny me food, or put me on a strict diet, the more I'd sneak into the kitchen for ice cream and cookies, and buy candy from school. It was a horrible, vicious cycle.''

''What about your father?'' Jack asked, and boosted himself up to sit on the stainless-steel countertop. ''Wasn't he around to witness all this?''

''When he was home from work, my father tried to make up for my mother's derogatory comments. But he really didn't have any idea just how bad it was.'' She realized just how much of her past she was revealing to Jack, more than she'd ever shared with anyone before. Opening herself up to him this way felt both liberating and frightening at the same time. ''And then when they divorced, my mother got full custody of both me and Jillian, and I only saw him during the summer months.''

He clasped his hands between his wide-spread thighs. "Where is your mother now?"

"She died a few years ago." An ending that had come with much relief, along with an enormous amount of pain because she'd never been able to please her mother. She'd often wondered if her mother would have been proud of the success she'd made of Pure Indulgence, or if she would have found a way to criticize her choice of career because of the way it would contribute to her weight problem.

She'd never know and, in a way, Kayla was glad, because her business was the one positive, reliable thing she could count on in her life. And she liked that it was hers, and hers alone, without any painful criticism or memories linked to it. There was more to her story, and since she'd come this far, she decided she ought to go for broke, to lay all the cards out on the table for Jack so he knew exactly what he was dealing with.

"As Jillian and I grew older, it wasn't just my mother who tried to pit us against each other emotionally. In high school, boys constantly compared the two of us and would ask me why I wasn't as hot as my sister, and why I was so fat when she was so skinny."

She drew a shuddering breath and risked a glance at Jack, who was waiting patiently for her to continue. "Needless to say, I didn't date much in high school, or even when I went off to college. The men I met were completely into physical looks, and I just didn't have what it took to turn their heads."

"I agree it's pretty shallow, but most guys in college are out for a fun time, not anything serious."

She concurred with his comment, but it didn't change the fact that a lack of self-confidence had been her constant companion during those years. It also made her wonder if that's how he felt about the women he dated. Women like Gretta. Fun and nothing serious.

If that was the case, what category did that put *her* into? *The category of women who seduced men with an aphrodisiac so outer appearances wouldn't matter*, her mind taunted.

"I guess at some point I got tired of being overlooked and missing out on all the fun." She crossed her arms over her chest, recognizing it for the defensive gesture it was, but she couldn't seem to help herself. "I went on a crash diet my senior year of college and I lost twenty pounds, and it was amazing the interest I attracted after that."

Her tone held a slight sarcastic note she couldn't hide. "That's when I met a guy named Doug, who was amazingly good-looking, charming, and totally into me. We dated for a year, until I gradually started gaining my weight back and he issued me an ultimatum to go on a diet, or we were through."

Jack visibly winced at Doug's thoughtless and uncompromising demand. "That was pretty crappy."

It had been devastating at the time, but a lesson learned. "Needless to say, that was the end of that relationship. I let my body stabilize at a weight I'm not constantly fighting and came to the decision that this is who I am and always will be, and I'm not about to change that for any man again."

"You shouldn't have to."

"No, you wouldn't think so, but so many of the men that I've met are looking for a beautiful, slender, sexy woman to have hanging on their arm."

He hopped down from the table and moved closer, his gaze holding hers. "You can't keep judging all men by the actions of a few, Kayla."

The underlying meaning to his words, his gentle voice, the intense look in his eyes made her want to believe that he was different.

"What about the women you date, like Gretta?" she said, and couldn't believe those words had slipped out of her mouth. But now that they were between them, she couldn't stop. "Can you deny that she's beautiful and slender and sexy? The perfect arm candy?"

Jack felt taken aback by Kayla's unexpected question, but could tell his answer was very important to her. To them. He considered his reply, knowing he had to tread carefully and not come on too strong, too soon, about his feelings for her. This was a fragile, vulnerable moment for Kayla, and since the emotions he was feeling were completely foreign to him, he hoped he was able to give her what she needed from him.

"On the outside, yes, Gretta is all those things." She glanced away, but not before he saw the pained look flash across her features.

Gently, he tucked his finger beneath her chin and brought her gaze back to his, forcing her to look deep into his eyes for the answers she sought. They were all there for her to see and find, if only she'd give him a chance.

"I've dated women like her because it was easy to maintain my distance and keep my emotions out of the relationship," he admitted, needing her to understand. "I knew they only wanted me for my money, and since I had no time for anything deeper in a relationship, women like Gretta were convenient and always around. But when you start looking for something real and lasting, you begin to look past the packaging and see what's inside. Gretta, like others, fell short there."

And that's exactly where he was in his life. Where he was with Kayla. Unfortunately she didn't understand he liked her body just fine and was equally taken by her generous heart.

Her gaze shimmied with confusion and hope, and he decided that he had to let her come to her own conclusions about herself, and them. That nothing he could say or do would ease those insecurities of hers. She had to trust in her feelings if she wanted things to work between them, and she had to trust in him. On her own, without his constant coaxing.

He let his hand fall away from her face, though he ached to draw her into his arms and kiss away every last one of her doubts. He knew if Jillian hadn't made her appearance at Pure Indulgence he would have made love to Kayla tonight. All the signs had been there, the desire and hunger. But now, after their serious conversation, it just wasn't the right time. She had things to think about, and so did he.

"What do you say we close up the shop and call it a night?" he suggested.

She nodded jerkily and stepped away from him. "That's a good idea."

He waited while she put away his file for Tremaine's Downtown in her office and returned with her purse and keys in hand. Together, they locked up the bakery and he walked her to her car. Once there, he opened the driver's door for her, then brushed a soft, chaste kiss across her lips that lingered longer than he'd intended.

God, not pulling her into a passionate embrace took every ounce of willpower he possessed.

He lifted his head, rubbed his hands up and down

her arms affectionately, and summoned a smile. "I'll see you Friday night for the art gallery show."

"Yes, see you then," she said softly, then slipped inside her vehicle.

Jack sat in his own car, watching the woman he was falling in love with drive away, and wondered if he'd done more harm than good with Kayla tonight.

He had one more night with her to find out.

9

JACK HEFTED his golf bag over his shoulder as he and Rich made their way over to the driving range to hit a bucket of practice balls. Jack desperately needed the release of smacking balls into oblivion to relieve the tension that had taken up residence in him since last night.

He exhaled a weary, confused sigh. His mind felt weighed down with emotions and fears he'd never experienced before—fears that Kayla wouldn't return the love he was beginning to harbor for her. Fears that he'd lose her because she wasn't ready to trust in him, or herself.

He was also worried that he wouldn't be able to give Kayla what she needed. He'd been alone and on his own for so long now, his previous relationships all deliberately shallow, that he found caring for another person was a scary prospect. It involved a range of feelings he was constantly sorting through, trying to figure out. He could give Kayla his love, his support in everything she did, but would that be enough to sway her, and ultimately keep her?

"Okay, Jack, how long is it going to take for you to finally tell me what's on your mind?" Rich's voice held traces of amusement, but his question was as straight-forward and candid as the man himself.

They reached the driving range, and Jack slanted his best friend a brief glance. "What makes you think I have anything on my mind?"

Rich laughed and shook his head incredulously as they each grabbed a club, their bucket of golf balls, and stepped up to the practice area. "I've known you way too long, buddy, and I know how to read you in a way few people do. First of all, you've been brooding all day long, and you've started this bizarre habit of invit-ing me to the driving range when you've got some-thing major on your mind."

Jack grunted in reply as he set a ball on a tee, certain that wasn't true at all.

Rich made a few practice swings before stepping up to his own ball. "Do you realize that all your important decisions over the past few years have been made out here on the range?"

Jack frowned. Did he really do that? "Yeah, like what decisions?"

"The first time was when you decided to give up your cheap two-bedroom apartment for a *real* house and mortgage. This is where you agonized over that decision," he pointed out wryly. "With me here, of course, listening to all the pros and cons of why you were finally ready to take that next step in your life."

Jack rolled his arms, trying to ease the taut muscles along his neck and shoulders before he lined up his shot. "One time doesn't make a habit."

"You're right. A habit does constitute more than once." Rich took a swing, and they both watched his ball fly one hundred and forty yards out, straight to the flag stick he'd been aiming at.

Rich turned to Jack with a cocky smile. "This is also the very place you decided to trade in your ten-year-old Dodge truck for your new Escalade. That was a huge, gut-wrenching decision for you."

He'd had that truck since high school and had seen no reason to replace it any sooner. "I'm a practical kind of guy," he said, feeling a bit defensive. "I don't like to spend money frivolously."

"Hell, I know that." Rich set another ball on his tee, but waited for Jack to take his first swing. "And I'm not criticizing your choice of thought process, just making you aware of the fact that this place seems to be where you do it best. In fact, the very last time we were here is when you made the decision to open a second restaurant."

All true, and Jack was amazed that he'd never seen the correlation himself. He swung and hit the ball, taking a huge divot out of the grass before sending the ball soaring to the right in the worst slice anyone had ever seen.

"Ahh, man," Rich said on a wince. "That shot sucked."

"Thank you for pointing that out to me."

"This is serious, isn't it?" Rich asked, much more concerned this time. "Usually your concentration is right on even while you're hashing out one of your decisions. Something's really got you shook up."

"I'm fine." And just to prove it, he took another shot and ended up topping the ball. He cursed beneath his breath.

"Come on, Jack. Just spill it," Rich said, putting his eight iron back in his bag in favor of a driver. "You'll feel a helluva lot better once you get whatever it is off your chest, and then we can go have a beer up at the clubhouse and toast to your newest acquisition."

This time was different. This was one time he couldn't just save up and purchase what he wanted. No, he had to earn it. And that was what made everything so uncertain, because the decision was out of his control.

Or was it?

The question nagged at Jack, and he transferred his gaze from the two-hundred-yard flag stick out on the range, to Rich. "It's Kayla Thomas."

Rich placed a ball on the tee. "I thought you said you were happy with the new dessert menu."

"I am."

Rich's brown eyes lit up. "Ahhh."

The one word held a wealth of understanding, and his friend just waited patiently for him to unload. "I'm falling in love with her." Jack scrubbed a hand over his jaw and finally admitted the truth out loud. "Hell, I'm already there."

"Congratulations," Rich said with a big grin. "You certainly have my blessing. I like her. A lot. And quite honestly, other than your crappy mood today, I can't remember the last time I've seen you so happy."

But Jack had a huge problem. He might be more content that he could ever remember being, but his biggest obstacle in getting what he wanted—a future with Kayla—was Kayla herself. And he had no idea how to get around her insecurities and emotional barriers.

"So, have you told her how you feel?" Rich asked while taking a few practice swings.

"No. Not yet."

Rich glanced his way with a frown. "Why not?"

"Because I'm afraid of scaring her away." He went on to explain a bit about Kayla's past to Rich, of how skittish she seemed to be of him and their developing relationship. And that he'd decided to take a step back and wait for her to come around on her own.

Rich took all that into consideration for a moment, then said, "In my opinion, you're taking the wrong approach with her."

Jack was willing to listen and learn, especially since Rich had more experience in the relationship department than he did—at least more experience with serious relationships that involved real emotion. While Jack had spent years keeping women at arm's length, Rich had been looking for that one special woman to spend his life with—but had yet to find her.

"I'm listening," Jack prompted.

"She's obviously not like all the other women you've dated," Rich said, and sent a golf ball soaring through the air in a clean, straight-line shot. "She's not demanding or assertive or overbearing."

"Not at all," Jack agreed. And those were some of the things that he loved about her. She wasn't at all smothering. She was gentle, sweet, and caring, and he was one-hundred-percent comfortable with her.

"So don't you think that since she doesn't possess any of those aggressive traits that she's going to read your signals all wrong? You're only making it easier for her to *let* you back off, because she thinks that's what you want." Rich selected a different club from his bag and briefly met Jack's gaze. "With you putting distance between the two of you, it's just going to reinforce her belief that you don't want someone like her."

His stomach cramped at the realization that Kayla might construe his actions in such a negative light. "I've never thought of it that way before."

"That's why I'm doing the talking, and you're doing the listening. And I'm not done yet." Rich lined up another shot. "For quite a while now, you've been dating women who were all wrong for you, whom you had no trouble keeping at arm's length. These women have been throwing themselves at you for so long that I'm thinking you've forgotten how to come on strong yourself, to make your intentions known. Now that you've found the right woman, you don't know how to open yourself up to her."

Jack was blown away by Rich's insight, and realized, in some ways, his friend knew him better than he understood himself. "You're right."

"Of course I'm right." The teasing note to Rich's voice tempered his arrogant comment. "The way I see things, you need to reassure her, Jack, so there's no second-guessing where you're coming from. Let her know how you feel, right up front. Get it out in the open and you can both deal with it in a straightforward, honest way."

How could he have been so stupid? So blind? Everything Rich said made sense, and eased that worry he'd felt about not being able to give Kayla what she needed in her life. He'd just required a bit of friendly advice from Rich to give him a sense of purpose with Kayla again.

"When are you seeing her again?" Rich asked.

"Tomorrow night." Setting a ball on his tee, Jack lined up his club, and eyed the one-hundred-and-sixty-yard flag stick, feeling calmer and more focused than he had in the past eighteen hours. "I'm going to an art show with her."

"Then there's your chance, buddy. After your date, tell her how you feel."

Jack was going to do exactly that, because he wasn't about to give Kayla the opportunity to shut him out. He had to put his own emotions on his sleeve if he expected her to do the same, and he was willing to take that first life-changing step with her. For her.

Jack swung his club, made perfect contact with the golf ball, and sent it sailing beyond the one-hundred-and-sixty-yard flag stick as if it had wings of its own.

Rich whistled long and low at Jack's powerful shot. "Looks like you're back in the game, buddy."

Jack flashed him a confident grin. "You better believe I am."

KAYLA HAD NEVER worn anything so daring and blatantly sexy, but she couldn't deny that she loved the sensual, confident way her new dress—a vivid purple, off-the-shoulder design—made her feel. With Jillian's guidance, she'd also bought a pair of two-inch heels that didn't make her stumble when she walked. That extra boost of height made her legs look longer, and more slender.

She'd worn her hair up, donned lacy lingerie and smoke-hued stockings, and dabbed perfume in all the right places. Tonight, she needed all the self-assurance she could muster to seduce Jack, because she had no idea what tomorrow would hold.

She'd tried her best to prepare herself for the end of their physical relationship. Other than deliveries of the desserts, which Kayla didn't do herself, they had no reason to see one another on a steady basis. After this evening, she'd be left to pick up the pieces of her shredded emotions.

But at least she'd have great memories to fall back on. They'd shared not just sex, which had been great, but an emotional bond that had helped her begin to gain some insight to herself, her past, and maybe even her future. And she intended to start that future by not having any regrets with Jack after this evening.

She had no time to contemplate further, because he arrived at her house to pick her up for the art show. He looked gorgeous in a black suit with a white shirt and gray patterned tie. Appearing surprisingly relaxed, he gave her a lazy smile of appreciation when he saw her.

She wasn't quite sure what to expect after their emotional conversation two nights ago, but one thing she knew for certain—she was ready for tonight. And she was ready for Jack.

Just as Jack parked the car in the Seaside Gallery parking lot and shut down the engine, and before he had a chance to exit the vehicle, Kayla opened up her purse and withdrew a small gold foil box.

"I brought a surprise for you," she said, and knew

by the dark heat in his eyes that he had a good idea what she held in her hands.

He rested his arm across the seat behind her and fingered a tendril of blond hair skimming the side of her neck. The contact made her shiver. "Dare I ask what's in that box you're holding?"

Just that quick, just that easily, her nipples puckered tight with need. Her candies were so unnecessary for her body to get primed and ready for him. No aphrodisiac would ever come close to duplicating the intense hunger that rippled through her at his knowing touch. Her desire for him was real, an all-encompassing combination of physical and emotional need.

Though she'd never be certain if the candies induced Jack's desire, she wasn't taking any chances with his libido tonight. It had been almost a week since they'd made love, and she ached for him in a way that transcended mere sex.

She wanted him desperately, needed him in a way she couldn't understand or explain. But she knew it had something to do with the emotions crowding her chest that told her she'd fallen much deeper than she'd intended and had given this man a piece of her heart in the process.

No one else had ever had the ability to make her nerve endings hum with such pleasure. No one had ever cared the way Jack did. But she'd seen his choice in women. And despite his protestations, she knew that was the kind of woman he wanted. After all, here she was, someone who looked nothing like his usual dates, and he hadn't tried to touch her in a week. So, if she had to return to her life before Jack, then she damn well was going to take advantage of everything tonight had to offer.

"I brought along a few Caramel Caresses, since you haven't tried them yet," she said, and moved the chocolates closer to him, hoping the sight of the candies' sensual shape would entice him.

He groaned, low and rough and sexy as hell. "You can't keep feeding me your candies," he said playfully, and trailed a finger along her bare shoulder. "You know what they do to me."

"Yeah, I do," she admitted out loud. That was the whole point of him eating them, she thought wryly.

Plucking a Caramel Caress from the box, she lifted it to his mouth and rolled the peaked tip against his bottom lip. "Open up and say ahhh," she teased.

He rolled his eyes, but did as she asked, and Kayla slid the chocolate into his mouth. *Finally.* He chewed, taking in the flavor and texture, and his brows rose in surprise.

"I was expecting just a caramel filling, but there's something else..." His voice trailed off as he attempted to figure out what the added taste was.

"It's a layer of creamy praline," she told him, and urged him to take another. "Do you like it?"

"Like everything else you've made, it's fantastic." He picked up a second piece of candy and bit it in half, then used his tongue to lick out the creamy, gooey center in a very provocative way.

Oh, God. Her insides quivered and she squirmed in her seat. She knew if they didn't get out of the car *now* she'd end up attacking him right then and there in the parking lot, the art event forgotten.

She ate one of the candies herself, put the lid back on the box, and set it on the center console for later. She'd given Jack more than enough of the aphrodisiac to spur a liberal amount of lust. Now it was just a matter of waiting for the right opportunity to present itself, so they could enjoy its effects.

They entered the Seaside Gallery and were greeted by Audrey. With her was Louis, the new artist whose paintings were being showcased for the special event. The place was filled with guests milling about, taking in the artwork on the walls, discussing the diverse sculptures on glass-topped tables, and viewing the featured artist's seascapes and marine life paintings. Kayla wasn't an art person, but was fascinated by the vibrant colors of the ocean and sunsets depicted on canvas. Jack seemed to be also.

She checked on the dessert table to make sure that everything looked as it should, and smiled as she overheard compliments from the guests on the *petits fours* and fondue sauces. She was thrilled when the employee serving the confections mentioned that the desserts had been supplied by Pure Indulgence.

"Champagne?" a young man asked as he held out a tray of drinks toward her and Jack.

"Umm, yes, please." Kayla took a flute of the bubbly liquid for herself, and passed one to Jack, too.

As they sipped their champagne, they strolled from room to room, discussing the artwork among themselves and with other guests. Jack remained by her side with his hand on the small of her spine, his touch possessive and arousing, as was the heat simmering in his eyes whenever their gazes met.

Every so often his palm would stroke lower, skimming provocatively over her bottom before returning to her back again. His illicit caresses made her breasts swell and her nipples peak, and intensified the desire pulsing between her thighs. She ached to touch him more intimately, too, to make him feel just as restless as she was, but they were surrounded by people and she was forced to behave herself. The necessity to practice restraint only served to elevate the hunger and need coiling tighter and tighter within her.

She finished off her champagne and set it on a passing tray just as they came across a sweeping staircase leading to a second level of the gallery. The entrance was roped off by a velvet cord, but that didn't stop Kayla from wanting to follow through on a mischievous idea that popped into her mind.

"Let's go see what's upstairs," she suggested in a whisper, excited by the prospect of being alone with Jack.

She expected a token protest from Jack, but he surprised her by agreeing, and like two naughty kids, they unlatched the velvet cord and quickly and silently made their way up to the second level.

It was quiet upstairs, and blessedly vacant. Hand in hand, they walked through the various rooms, taking in artwork that was more exotic and titillating than what was displayed below. Abstracts of nudes adorned the walls, along with real-life sketches and paintings that ranged from subtly sensual to more blatantly erotic.

"Take a look at these," Jack said in a low, astonished tone of voice.

He tugged her into a small room that was dimly lit, with marbled columns displaying a collection of bronze sculptures of nude couples in various sexual positions—from the standard missionary pose, to a man taking a woman from behind, to a woman sitting on top of a man. Fascinated and feeling like a voyeur in the midst of an orgy, Kayla stepped closer to a different pair of sculptures and was shocked to discover that each one depicted a couple being pleasured orally.

The first one portrayed a woman on her knees in front of a man, taking his shaft into her mouth while he twined his fingers through her long hair. His head was thrown back in the throes of ecstasy, his muscled body taut and straining, his face reflecting a passion so strong Kayla felt it to the very core of her being.

And then there was another of a woman lying on her back, her naked body arched and her hands caressing her own breasts as the man between her spread legs pleasured her with his tongue.

Jack came up behind her, rested his hands on her bare shoulders, and skimmed his lips close to her ear.

"That's exactly what I want to do to you."

His soft, seductive voice curled through her belly and sent shivers skittering across her skin. There was no denying the dampness gathering between her thighs at the thought of him pleasuring her so intimately, so erotically. Her sex felt heavy and swollen, her entire body strung tight with an urgent, demanding need she could no longer suppress.

She turned around and searched his dark, masculine features, taking in the desire that was for her alone. The fire she saw in his eyes made her weak in the knees and eager to experience anything and everything he was willing to offer tonight—even something as forbidden as an illicit tryst among erotic sculptures.

"*Yes,*" she murmured. Curling her hand around his neck, she brought his mouth down to hers for a kiss that was deep and hot and wild.

With a low growl that reverberated in his chest, he pressed her up against the nearest wall and aligned his body to hers. His hands slipped down her sides, past her bottom and thighs, his touch urgent and wondrously aggressive, spurring her to a greater level of anticipation.

Grasping the hem of her dress, he shoved it up to her waist, exposing her lower body to the cool air in the room. She barely had time to catch her breath before he hooked his fingers behind one knee and lifted her leg up to his hip so that he could press his groin to hers. She felt every single hard inch of him.

She whimpered against his lips and shamelessly rubbed the hottest, neediest part of her against his thick shaft. Just as she'd shed all of her inhibitions, she wanted the flimsy barrier of her panties gone, too.

Jack seemed to know exactly what she needed, what she desperately craved. He sank to the carpeted floor in front of her and rasped, "Hold your dress up for me."

Caught up in the moment, she did as he asked. She gripped the silky fabric in tight fists, her thighs quivering as he dragged her underwear down and off, shoved them into his coat pocket, then smoothed his palms upward. He eased her legs further apart so he could touch her slick flesh with his long, warm fingers and could look his fill of her, which he did without an ounce of concern for her own modesty.

Kayla's heart slammed in her chest, and she couldn't move, couldn't seem to breathe as she waited for the decadent pleasure he'd promised her. Everywhere she looked she was surrounded by carnal images, and in her mind those sculptures became her and Jack, entwined in hedonistic positions, doing deliciously wicked things to one another...

"God, you're so, so beautiful," he said in an ardent whisper that touched her heart in unexpected ways, despite the sexual intensity of the moment.

She loved his tenderly spoken words, loved the way he made her feel beautiful and sexy when she was with him. He stroked along her cleft in a slow, maddening rhythm, and her hips moved helplessly against the glide of his fingers, his touch teasing instead of fulfilling the way she needed them to. "Jack...*please*."

He rubbed his cheek against her thigh, his lips warm and damp on her skin. "Shhh...I'll give you what you need, sweetheart."

His thumbs skimmed her swollen lips, opening her to him so that he could kiss her, deeply and intimately. His hot breath, the suctioning swirl of his tongue, all combined to make her come in a blinding, gut-wrenching rush of sensation completely beyond anything she'd ever experienced before. A low, sobbing cry escaped her throat, and her trembling legs threatened to give out on her.

He stood up, pinning her against the wall with the strength of his hard, aroused body. His lips claimed hers in a slow, lazy kiss that gave her time to come down from the exquisite high of her climax.

He drew back minutes later, when she could finally think and breath normally again, and gently touched her face. "You're amazing, you know that?"

She smiled drowsily, physically sated for the moment.

"I think you get all the credit for what just happened here, but I'd like to think that I can do amazing things to you, too." She smoothed her hand down his chest and cupped his erection in her palm.

He groaned like a dying man and grasped her wrist to stop her purposeful strokes. "Not here," he said huskily. "I want to take this somewhere private. Let's say goodbye to the host and get the hell out of here."

Kayla wasn't about to argue.

10

AS SOON AS THEY WALKED into Kayla's house and the door was closed behind them, she was all over Jack, in an aggressive, demanding way that initially caught him off guard.

This time, she had *him* pressed up against the nearest wall, her mouth wild and greedy on his as she pushed his coat from his shoulders and nearly ripped open the buttons on his shirt in her haste to get it off him. She flattened her palms on his chest, over his rigid nipples, then dragged her cool fingers all the way down to the waistband of his slacks. She slanted her mouth beneath his, taking the kiss to a deeper, more erotic level as her shaking hands worked to loosen his belt, then fumbled to unbutton his slacks.

Her movements were anxious and eager, with a frantic edge that went beyond passion and touched on a desperation that made him wonder at its source. She was attacking him as if she feared he'd change his mind about them. As if this was the last time they'd ever make love.

Neither worries were even a distinct possibility, and

he sought to ease her reckless, frenzied actions because he intended for this night to last longer than the time it took for a quick release. And that's exactly where things were heading if they didn't take tonight at a more leisurely pace.

He gently captured her face in his hands and pulled her head back a few inches, so he could look into her eyes. The entryway was dark and shadowed, but there was no mistaking the flush on her cheeks and the barely concealed glimmer of emotion in her gaze. "Slow down, Kayla, sweetheart. I'm not going anywhere."

She gave her head a quick shake in what seemed too much like a denial. "I need you inside me."

"That's exactly where I want to be, too," he said, and slid his thumbs along her jawline in a tender, calming caress. "We'll get there, I promise."

Their last two sexual encounters had been frenzied and quick, with their clothes barely shoved out of the way. Tonight was too important to him and to their relationship to rush. This time he wanted them both naked, wanted to feel her skin against his, wanted to see and watch the way her body responded to the touch of his hands, the stroke of his mouth.

And mostly, he wanted to make love to her on a soft mattress, face-to-face, heartbeat to heartbeat. "Take me to your bedroom."

She hesitated, just long enough for him to decide to

take matters into his own hands. Lacing his fingers through hers, he moved down the darkened hallway, past what appeared to be an office she'd set up at home, until he found her bedroom. He pulled her inside, then moved to turn on the lamp on the nightstand.

"Jack, don't."

The panic in her voice stopped him before he could flood the room with light. He wasn't surprised to hear her quivering demand, and told himself to be patient. He'd have to tackle one issue at a time with Kayla, no matter how badly he wanted to see her without a stitch of clothing on, all soft planes and luscious curves for him to gaze upon.

Tonight he'd have to be satisfied with stripping her completely naked by the light of a moonbeam streaming through the window. He'd give her that tonight, and tomorrow he'd tell Kayla he'd fallen in love with her. Slow, intimate steps designed to build her trust in him. To let her know that he wanted more than an affair with her, more than sex in the dark. He wanted a commitment, a future, and he wanted that with her. And that meant no hiding anything—not even her body.

"Come here," he said softly, and waited for her to join him by the edge of the bed, then pulled the pins from her hair and let the wavy tresses fall to her shoulders. "Now turn around so I can unzip your dress."

She did as he asked, and he brushed his lips along the side of her neck as he lowered the zipper down to her spine, then unhooked the clasp on her bra. He felt her shiver as he smoothed the sleeves of her dress down her arms, and pushed the rest of the material over her hips so it fell to the floor and out of his way.

He eased her back around again and grew excruciatingly hard at what he'd uncovered. Since he'd taken off her panties earlier, she stood before him in nothing but smoke-hued stockings that ended with a feminine band of lace at mid thigh. He took in the dark shadow between her legs, the swell of her hips silhouetted by moonlight, and the full breasts that balanced the shape of her body perfectly.

He reached out to touch her tense jaw. He could see in her eyes that, even in the darkness, she couldn't bring herself to shed her doubts about herself, about her lush body, which was his every fantasy come to life.

He smoothed his fingers along her jaw to her chin. "You have no reason to be uncomfortable with me, so let it go," he murmured gently. "Especially here and now."

Something shimmered in her eyes, the barest hint of hope, and much to his wonder her slight resistance faded. Without him asking, she scooted on top of the bed and lay there, silently waiting for him to join her.

After quickly removing his slacks and briefs, he

sheathed himself with a condom, then moved to a position by her feet, determined to make this experience one she wouldn't soon forget. Grasping the lacy band hugging her thigh, he slowly, leisurely stripped off one stocking, then the other, letting his fingers trail sensuously along the back of her knee and over her smooth calves as he peeled away the silky fabric.

Then he began kissing his way upward, relying on his senses of taste and touch to make up for his lack of sight. He used the lazy glide of his hands, the damp heat of his mouth, and the soft stroke of his tongue to blaze a fiery trail along her parted thighs.

She said his name on a breathless, plaintive sigh and clutched the bedcovers in her fists when he finally pushed one finger, then two, deep inside her creamy center and put his mouth right where she needed the pressure of his tongue the most.

She came almost instantly, bucking against his mouth, and her moan of pleasure meshed with his as he took her higher still, until she begged him to please, please stop. He did, but only because he'd yet to skim his lips over the curve of her hip, the softness of her stomach. She writhed as he dipped his tongue into her navel, and her fingers tangled in his hair to urge him up.

He deliberately took his time, refusing to be rushed, and gradually made his way up to her voluptuous breasts. He laved her nipples, traced the swell of her cleavage with his tongue, and grazed the plump flesh with his teeth. She squirmed beneath him, whimpering fretfully.

Long minutes later, he kneed her thighs wider apart and moved over her so that his throbbing erection was nestled against the lips of her sex. Entwining their fingers, he pinned her hands at the side of her head. When they were finally face-to-face, heartbeat to heartbeat, then, and only then, did he thrust deep, stretching her, filling her, his penetration so powerful and complete that they both moaned simultaneously.

But still, it wasn't enough. "Wrap your legs high around my waist," he said.

She did, her thighs clasping his hips and her ankles locked at the base of his spine. The position caused her bottom to lift, her hips to tilt, and he buried himself to the very base of his shaft.

"*Oh, yeah,*" he growled. He slowly ground against her as he trailed hot, openmouthed kisses along her jaw, her throat, and then gave her a love bite on her neck.

She sobbed in frustration, her body arching, straining against him, trying to urge him to a wilder rhythm. In his own sweet time he eventually gave her what she wanted, gradually surging faster, harder, deeper, until both of their bodies submitted to the inevitable...a glorious, stunning climax that drained them both.

As the tremors faded, he lowered his mouth to

Kayla's and kissed her, their bodies still joined, and the beat of her heart matching his. He let go of her hands and touched her face, and everything within him went still as he felt something wet against his fingertips. Even without the lights on, he knew exactly what that moisture was, and all he could do was pray they were tears of joy, not regret.

KAYLA WOKE UP alone in her bed, but the sounds coming from the kitchen assured her that Jack was still there. Smiling drowsily and with more contentment than she could ever remember feeling, she stretched beneath the covers, completely naked and thoroughly sated—her body, heart and soul.

She sighed, remembering the way Jack had held her so intimately during the course of the night, never letting her stray very far before he'd pull her back against the heat of his body and snuggle close. Kayla had to admit that she loved the feel of his warm, strong arms around her, of having him cradle her as if he never wanted to let her go. And despite knowing that the morning could quite possibly bring heartache, she'd reveled in his attention and affection.

Because she loved him. Kayla swallowed hard as she forced herself to acknowledge the overwhelming, terrifying emotion she never expected to become a part of her affair with Jack. She'd set out to enjoy a sexual relationship, and to test her aphrodisiac candies on a hot, sexy guy. But in no way had she believed it could lead to something more.

Yes, she had. Kayla couldn't lie to herself anymore. The entire time she'd been intent on seducing Jack, she'd allowed herself to be seduced by him in return. Not just her body, but her emotions, as well.

Her heart squeezed tight in her chest. She had no one to blame but herself for letting her emotions become involved in her affair with Jack. Her candies might have spurred his lust and interest in her, but she knew without a doubt that they weren't responsible for the way she felt about him. Her emotions were real—*too damn real*—and while she ached for something more, he'd never promised her anything beyond what they'd shared. And since she'd gone into this relationship without any expectations, she had to leave it the same way.

A part of her had instinctively known all that last night, hence the tears that had fallen before she could stop them.

The sound of coffee percolating, followed by the tantalizing aroma drifting into her bedroom told her it was time to get up and moving. To get dressed and face the morning, and whatever it might bring.

WHILE THE COFFEE FINISHED brewing, Jack searched the refrigerator for something to make for breakfast. First they'd eat, then they'd talk. They had a whole lot to discuss, and he figured it was better to do it on a full stomach, rather than an empty one.

After last night, telling Kayla how he felt about her seemed as natural as breathing. He hoped it would be just as easy for her to believe. He might not have told her verbally that he was in love with her, but there had been an undeniable emotional connection between them that should have left no doubt in her mind that he cared deeply about her.

He found eggs, bread to make some toast, and a half of a cantaloupe. Perfect. He set the items on the kitchen counter and pushed aside one of those gold boxes of candies that Kayla was always feeding him, along with a file folder that was in his way. A few of the papers slid out, and he automatically tucked them back inside the folder. The words written on the file tab caught his eye, and his attention: Aphrodisiac Candies.

Undeniably intrigued, he opened the folder. The lined papers were filled with handwritten recipes, all of which he recognized as the candies Kayla had been feeding him over the course of the past few weeks: Heavenly Kisses, Love Bites, Chocolate Orgasms, and Caramel Caresses.

Frowning in confusion, he withdrew a package of a white powdery substance and read the information on the label, which included a statement that made him go very still inside: *Aphrodisiac for lovers. An all-natural stimulant guaranteed to increase your sex drive and bring out the lust and passion in the one you desire.*

He shook his head in stunned disbelief, certain he'd misread the fine print. Unfortunately, a second glance did nothing to change the meaning of the words on the package, and everything it implied.

He swore beneath his breath, more than a little upset at what he'd just discovered. Yes, Kayla had told him right up front that she wanted his opinion on the new line of candies she was considering for Pure Indulgence, and he'd actually enjoyed sampling her more erotic creations. But she obviously hadn't divulged her hidden agenda. He'd been nothing more than an experiment for her.

The evidence against her was glaring, and he held the proof of her deceit in his hands. While he hated thinking that everything they'd shared had all been part of some elaborate plan he couldn't help but hope there was some kind of logical explanation.

"Good morning."

Kayla's soft morning voice pulled him out of his turbulent thoughts, and he turned around to face her. She stood just inside the kitchen doorway, her hair slightly tousled, her skin flushed from a night of great sex, and she was wearing a silky robe that made her look extremely sensual and damn appealing. If he hadn't discovered this incriminating evidence, which definitely required an immediate explanation, he would have stripped off that flimsy garment and made love to her again this morning, right here in the damn kitchen.

But he wasn't about to allow anything to distract him from finding out the truth about those candies she'd been feeding him.

"Morning," he replied evenly. Forgetting about his breakfast plans, he indicated the open folder on the counter that revealed her secret recipes. "What's this?"

She sucked in a startled breath, her eyes widening with a glimmer of panic.

"I..." She shifted on her feet, swallowed hard, and tried again. "Umm, those are the recipes for the new line of candies I'm considering for Pure Indulgence."

"I gathered as much," he said, unable to keep the wry tone out of his voice, which was a helluva lot tamer than the anger welling inside him. "I've been lucky enough to have sampled each one of these candies. But it's not the candies I'm questioning, but rather what you've been putting *in* them. According to these recipes, it appears you've come up with some very interesting concoctions. And I'm assuming you fed them to me as some sort of experiment?" The thought made his stomach cramp.

She winced, obviously knowing exactly what he was referring to. But to her credit, she didn't lie or try to play dumb like most of the women he'd known would have attempted to do.

"Yes," she whispered, looking mortified. "I wanted

to know if that aphrodisiac I bought really worked, so I asked you to eat the candies so I could gauge your re-action to the sexual stimulant.''

He couldn't believe what he was hearing. Couldn't comprehend the possibility that she believed in such ridiculous nonsense. ''And what kind of conclusion did you come to with these candies and my reaction to them, Kayla?'' he asked, curious to know what she thought she'd accomplished.

She glanced away from his intense stare, her fingers toying anxiously with the hem of her robe. ''You were definitely seduced by the candies and what was in them.''

He crossed his arms over his chest, not caring for where the direction of this conversation was heading, or what she was insinuating. ''No, I was seduced by *you*,'' he replied succinctly.

''You might think that's true,'' she said softly, an aching vulnerability lacing her voice, ''but, in all hon-esty, it was most likely the aphrodisiac that, well, prompted your response to me.''

''Look at me,'' he ordered. Even from across the room he wanted her to look in his eyes and see the truth for herself. Once her gaze tentatively met his again, he said in a steady tone, ''I was not at all influ-enced by your candies.''

''I know it might be hard for you to believe, but it's true.'' Her chin lifted a mutinous notch. ''Those candies are responsible for every time we've been together sexually.''

Frustration rode him hard. Good God, she wasn't serious, was she? But one look at her adamant expression and he knew that she truly believed her candies were the reason he'd made love to her those times. ''Give me enough credit to know the difference between real passion and fabricated lust, and I resent the fact that you think I need some kind of sexual stimulant to want you.''

She didn't back down from her claim. ''The first time we kissed was right after you'd eaten a few Heavenly Kisses,'' she said, ticking off with her fingers. ''Then you ate the Love Bites the night you cooked dinner for me here and we ended up having sex at the kitchen table. But the most telling proof I have of those candies and the power they have to induce lust and desire is the time I sent you the Chocolate Orgasms at your restaurant. Do you remember what happened?''

''Jesus, Kayla, how could I forget?'' He shoved his fingers through his hair impatiently, wondering if there was any way to convince her that his desire for her was real, and always had been, and had absolutely nothing to do with her enhanced desserts. ''After eating those Chocolate Orgasms I wanted you in the worst way, but not because of some kind of stimulant. I wanted you because while I was eating those candies

I was thinking of you and what we'd done together the night before, and it turned me on. *You* turn me on."

"Then how do you explain all the times when we could have had sex and didn't, and each one of those times you didn't eat any of my aphrodisiac candies?"

He wanted to howl in frustration. He wanted to shake some sense into her. "It was nothing more than a coincidence."

She shook her head sadly, as if she wished that were true. "No, it wasn't. I've felt the reaction of those candies."

"Have you really?" he drawled incredulously. "And what, exactly, have you felt?"

"Warm. Tingly. Amorous." She shrugged her shoulders, causing that silky material to shift and slide over her full, generous breasts. "It happens every time I eat those candies."

He still wasn't buying it. He just couldn't suspend his disbelief that way...until it dawned on him why she was clinging so steadfastly to her claim that those candies were responsible for him wanting her. Because she couldn't bring herself to believe that he was sexually attracted to her on his own.

Her past with her mother and Doug had instilled her with the impression that without a slim, svelte body no man would give her a second glance. And those deeply rooted insecurities had prompted her to create her candies, and to believe in their power of persuasion when it came to his desire for her.

Those candies also protected her emotions, he realized. In her mind, when their affair ended, instead of facing the kind of rejection her mother and Doug had put her through, she could cling to the excuse that the aphrodisiac was the reason he'd lusted after her. And without those candies, his desire had waned.

He understood her motives, maybe better than she did. But he hated that she couldn't believe that he wanted her for who and what she was beyond surface appearance.

He figured there was only one way to convince her that those laced candies didn't have a friggin' thing to do with him wanting her. His feelings for her were as real as he was flesh and blood, and she was about to discover that for herself. In this case, his actions *would* speak louder than the words she didn't want to listen to.

He moved across the room toward her...slowly and easily, because she'd suddenly turned wary as he approached. "Since you've used me as your guinea pig the past few weeks, I'm going to conduct a little experiment of my own, and I expect your full cooperation in return."

Uncertainty shone in her eyes, but she didn't refuse him. "All right."

"Take note. I haven't had any candies this morning,"

he said, then slid his fingers to the back of her head and brought her mouth to his.

She initially stiffened, apparently not sure what his intentions were. He kissed her slowly at first, then gradually drew her into a deeper, hotter melding of lips and tongues that made her moan low in her throat. He felt her posture soften along with her mouth and used that opportunity to slip an arm around her back and bring her body flush to his. He cupped her breast in his hand, found her nipple through the silk of her robe and lightly pinched the taut tip.

Her breathing deepened, and so did his. Still kissing her, he smoothed his palm over her bottom then trailed his fingers up her thigh, beneath the hem of her robe, until he encountered the damp heat of her desire for him.

She shuddered in his arms, a soft whimper of need escaping her lips.

Now it was her turn to feel his passion, too.

Grasping one of her wrists, he eased her hand between their bodies and molded her fingers over the fierce erection straining against the fly of his slacks. There was no denying how she affected him physically, that his response was as real as it got. And if this wasn't enough proof for her, then he didn't know what else to do.

He lifted his mouth from hers, still holding her hand against his aching shaft, and stared into her dark green

eyes. "This has nothing to do with any goddamn aphrodisiac, Kayla," he said, his tone rough with arousal.
"It has everything to do with *you*, the woman I've
fallen in love with."

She inhaled a quick, startled gasp of astonishment,
seemingly rendered speechless by his declaration.

He hadn't meant for the words to come out that way,
in the middle of a heated argument. But there was no
better time to set her straight about how he felt about
her, and so he just went with the moment and what
was in his heart.

"That's right, Kayla," he said, softer now. "I'm in
love with you. And I thought that you felt something
for me, too."

"Oh, God...I do."

"Do you?" He couldn't read her expression, not
enough to assure him of her true emotions. "Are you
sure it's real and not the candies making you feel and
think that way?"

He was mocking her, tossing back her own theory
about her aphrodisiac candies. And she was confused
enough not to answer his question, which told him she
still had to come to terms with her insecurities and
emotions before they could take this relationship any
further.

But before he left, there were a few things he still
needed to say and wanted her to hear. He let her go,

then took a step back, putting distance between them again.

"I just showed you what you do to me without any kind of stimulant, and now you know that I'm in love with you. When I look at you I see a beautiful, sensual woman who has so much to give, emotionally and physically...if only you'd have faith in yourself."

He steeled himself against the tears welling in her eyes, the fear and panic he saw there that wrenched at his heart. "I want a future with you. I want your body, your mind and your heart. I want the whole package. You are who you are, Kayla, but you have to trust that my feelings are genuine, and not a fabrication of some kind of bizarre aphrodisiac. And when you can do that, then you know where to find me."

He walked out of the kitchen while he still had the will to do so and quickly gathered up his things. Minutes later he was gone, knowing there was a good chance he'd just lost the only woman he'd ever truly loved.

11

KAYLA WAS SO IMMERSED in her baking and her misery that she didn't hear Jillian enter her house until her sister was standing in her kitchen. Kayla turned from pulling a sheet of sticky pecan rolls from the oven and nearly dropped the pan on the floor in surprise.

"Damn it, Jillian," she grumbled as she slid the pan onto a cooling rack she'd set up on the table. At this point, it was just about the only vacant space left in her entire kitchen, which was currently filled with an abundance of cakes, pies, and other desserts. "Could you at least let me know you're here before you barge in and scare the living daylights out of me?"

"Hello to you, too," Jillian greeted her, unfazed by her grouchy mood. "And for your information, I knocked twice before letting myself into the house. Considering your employees told me that you haven't been to the shop in two days, and I haven't heard from you either, I thought I'd check up on you."

Kayla shoved a pound cake into the oven to bake and tossed her oven mitts on the counter. "I'm fine."

"Okay," Jillian said in a placating tone as she

strolled through the kitchen and eyed the various sweets lining the countertops. "What's with all this?" The wave of her sister's hand encompassed the array of treats.

Kayla stirred the ingredients for a carrot cake, beating the batter longer and harder than necessary. "I'm working at home."

"You haven't baked at home like this since before you opened Pure Indulgence," Jillian commented thoughtfully. She picked up an Almond Joy Cookie and took a bite of the chewy chocolate and coconut confection. "In fact, the last time I remember your kitchen being an explosion of desserts was when I came home from New York for a visit after things ended between you and Doug."

Kayla winced at her sister's too-intuitive speculation. Baking was not only Kayla's livelihood, but she'd discovered long ago that it was also therapeutic when she needed to release stress, tension, or anger. In this case, though, she was baking up a storm to keep her mind off Jack and to keep her emotional grief at bay.

So far, her therapy wasn't working worth a damn.

"So, are you going to tell me what's going on, or am I going to have to tickle it out of you?" Jillian waggled her fingers at Kayla threateningly.

Despite her heartache, Kayla laughed at her sister's attempt at intimidation—another childhood antic they'd made up as kids when they wanted to extract important information from one another. Jillian was a ruthless tickler and always managed to persuade Kayla to spill her guts.

She inhaled a deep breath, and let it out slowly. "Jack and I...well, it's over."

"Over?" her sister echoed, her expression almost as devastated as Kayla felt deep inside. "What do you mean, *over?*"

"Not our business relationship," she explained, just in case Jillian thought that's what she meant. "Our affair."

Jillian's gaze narrowed and she braced her hands on her slender hips, her entire demeanor going into protective mode, even though she was the younger of the two of them. "Maybe I ought to go and have a talk with Mr. Tremaine," she said haughtily. "No one hurts my sister and gets away with it—"

"Settle down, Jilly," Kayla said, knowing her sister wouldn't hesitate to confront Jack on her behalf. "It wasn't him. It was...me. I'm the one who let things end."

Jillian's shoulders slumped, and she reached for a brownie on a nearby plate. "But why?"

Kayla turned around and poured the carrot cake batter into a pan, unable to bring herself to explain the whole aphrodisiac candy situation to her sister and unwilling to end up sounding like a complete fool. "I guess Doug did a bigger number on my confidence than I realized."

"Doug was an idiot and you can't compare every man to him," Jillian said from behind her.

Jack had told her the same thing the night he'd come to her shop to taste the cheesecakes.

"I have to tell you," Jillian said went on, "if you let Jack go without a fight, then *you're* being the idiot."

Leave it to her sister to be blunt, Kayla thought as she scraped the last of the batter into the pan. But as each minute of each hour of each day passed by and a deeper loneliness settled within her, she was inclined to believe that she was very much an idiot for allowing Jack to walk out her door two mornings ago.

Except she was having a difficult time getting past the fears and insecurities that kept her and her aching heart in their relentless grip.

Unable to turn around and face her sister, she squeezed her eyes shut, summoned an extra boost of fortitude, and admitted, "I'm scared, Jilly. Scared to believe in something so good."

"I know," she said, a deep understanding in her tone. "But aren't you more afraid of losing such a great guy?"

Kayla's throat closed up with emotion, cutting off her ability to speak. But the words still came, filtering effortlessly through her mind. Yes, she was petrified of losing Jack, which was part of the problem, too. Going after Jack meant taking a big risk...the risk that he might eventually end things with her. The resulting heartache and overwhelming sense of rejection could devastate her.

Yet she was beginning to accept and understand that loving Jack meant taking that risk and trusting him enough to believe that he'd never intentionally hurt her that way.

"Oh my God, Kayla!" Jillian exclaimed appreciatively. "These candies are *fabulous*. What are they?"

Jolted back to the present, Kayla whirled around and found her sister eating the leftover Caramel Caresses that Kayla hadn't touched since Jack had left her house. Her first instinct was to snatch the box out of her sister's hands and berate her for helping herself to something she had no business eating.

Instead of freaking out over this interesting turn of events, Kayla watched her sister consume another piece of the candy and decided to gauge her reaction to the Caramel Caresses. "Those are part of the new line of candies I'm creating for Pure Indulgence."

"Wow, they're very yummy." Jillian examined another piece closer. "You know, the shape of the candies kind of reminds me of a woman's breast."

"They're meant to look that way, to add to the sensuality of the candy." Kayla washed her sticky hands and dried them on a terry towel, but kept her gaze on her sister, who popped that third candy into her mouth and was chewing blissfully. "Jillian...do you feel anything at all?"

"Feel anything, like what?" Jillian asked, clearly confused as to what Kayla was suggesting.

Kayla recalled all the sensations those aphrodisiac candies had induced in her when she'd eaten them. "Warm. Tingly. Maybe a little...turned on?"

A frown creased Jillian's brows. "Are you having a nervous breakdown?"

"No." Kayla bit her bottom lip, looking for some kind of external sign that her sister was affected by those candies, but found none. "So, you don't feel anything sexual at all?" she persisted, needing to know.

"Look, I don't know what's gotten into you, but you're crazy for thinking a piece of chocolate, or two or three, can send a person's hormones into a frenzy. If that were the case, half the world's population would be walking around, completely turned on all the time."

Realizing that her sister truly wasn't affected by her candies, Kayla experienced a mingled rush of disappointment and relief. Disappointment because her exciting idea to start a new line of aphrodisiac candies at Pure Indulgence wasn't going to happen and she'd have to rethink her strategy with those new confections, and a huge surge of relief because the truth had just set a part of her free.

Free to believe, free to trust, free to love.

And most importantly, free to be herself.

"Why are you asking me these questions, anyway?" Jillian asked as she licked off smudges of caramel from her fingers.

"Because I put an aphrodisiac into those candies, and I needed to know if you had any kind of reaction to them."

Jillian was shocked, but became even more so when Kayla went on to explain that she'd used Jack for her experiment, and that she'd believed that every time they'd made love had been because of those candies.

She'd even fooled herself into believing her own libido had been affected by the stimulant. But it had all been in her mind.

Now Kayla understood what she couldn't bring herself to face that last morning with Jack. She'd wanted so badly to arouse Jack's passion that she'd read more into his sexual advances, certain they stemmed from an aphrodisiac.

The power of suggestion had been strong, her will to believe in something so mystical even stronger because she'd always wanted a man to desire her as intently, as completely, as Jack had when he'd eaten those candies. But she'd never believed it possible.

Jillian grasped Kayla's hand, directing her attention back to her. "Kayla, Jack Tremaine is absolutely crazy about you," she said with a smile. "I saw the way he looked at you that night at the shop when I interrupted the two of you. The whole time I was talking to him he was watching *you* move around the kitchen. What he feels for you is the real thing.''

Finally, Kayla knew that, too. But was she too late to make amends?

''I know that the way Mother treated you, and Doug, too, is a big reason why you find it so hard to believe that a man like Jack can accept all of you, but it *can* happen. Don't let those damn voices in your head prevent you from moving on with your life. I know you're afraid of putting your emotions out there in the open and facing the possibility of rejection, but some things are worth risking.''

And Jack was definitely worth the risk, she knew. ''When did you become so smart?'' Kayla teased.

''Trust me, there are plenty of brains beneath this blond hair,'' she said with a sassy toss of her head. ''And we've both been in relationships that have played hell on our confidence and self-esteem, so I understand how you feel. But despite being burned before, I do believe that there's someone out there for everyone. A soul mate who'll love us for who we are inside. And I'm thinking maybe you've found yours in Jack.''

Jillian's words were so profound, so full of hope and determination that Kayla found herself believing in true love and happily-ever-afters—for herself *and* Jillian.

And as Kayla gazed at her sister, she realized that

despite how slender and beautiful and sophisticated Jillian was, she was just as capable of being hurt, and she'd had her own insecurities to bear, just like any other woman. It just underlined that a person was a lot more than what they showed on the outside.

Which was what Jack had been trying to tell Kayla all along.

Her relationship with Jack had never been based on her weight or body image. That had been her hang-up, her insecurity. And Kayla supposed her decision about whether or not to let Jack into her life was based on a question that every woman, no matter what size or shape, had to ask herself at some point...was she willing to take a risk with her emotions and trust another person with her heart?

Kayla's answer came without hesitation. She was ready and willing to take whatever risks were necessary to have Jack in her life. Even if it meant baring herself to him—heart, body and soul.

CHIN HELD HIGH with every ounce of confidence she possessed, and her heart hammering wildly in her chest, Kayla knocked on the front door of Jack's house. A big, gorgeous, custom-made home that overlooked the ocean and was a testimony to all of Jack's hard work and resulting success over the past years.

She knew he was home, not only because of the Escalade parked in the circular drive, but because she'd gone to Tremaine's Downtown to look for him, only to be told he'd taken the night off. His friend and manager, Rich, had been kind enough to give her his home address, along with a promise that Jack would be thrilled to see her.

Except when Jack opened the door wearing nothing but a pair of navy-blue cotton sweatpants, he didn't look overjoyed to find her standing on his porch. Surprised, yes. Thrilled, no. He stared at her with an uncertainty that made her own chest tighten with a wealth of dread. Most prominent was the fear that he'd changed his mind about her.

Her confidence faltered, but her sister's convictions along with her own—which had replaced those other more destructive voices in her head—now helped her to stay strong. She refused to leave until she set the record straight with Jack about her feelings for him.

"Come on in," he said, and held the door open wider for her to enter.

She walked inside a large foyer, accepting his invitation as a very positive sign. She turned around to face him again and attempted to explain her presence.

"Rich gave me your address and directions—"

"I don't give a damn how you found my place," he said, his voice low and rough, his expression unreadable. "I'm just glad you're here."

Glad...but not thrilled. They were getting there, slowly but surely.

"Come on in," he said again. After shutting the front door, he led the way into a spacious living room.

"Make yourself comfortable," he said, gesturing toward the sofa and love seat. "Would you like something to drink?"

"No, thank you. I'm fine." He was treating her like a casual acquaintance—not that she could really blame him considering the way things had ended between them.

And now she was back, barging into his life, hoping and praying she wasn't too late to make amends. Hoping and praying that what she had to offer him would be enough to earn back his trust. His love. For a lifetime.

He settled himself on the couch, those broad shoulders and strong chest of his momentarily distracting her from her original purpose. Desire settled warm and low in her belly, and that tingling sensation spreading through her veins was pure sexual attraction, an all-natural, aphrodisiac-free lust.

It was a wonderful, glorious feeling.

"Kayla?" he prompted, tipping his head curiously. "Are you going to tell me why you're here?"

There were so many reasons why she'd come. So many things she needed to say and share with him. And there was one very important facet of who she was that she needed to show him.

First, she'd start with baring her soul.

"I want to apologize about the candies," she began, and because she was feeling too restless to sit, she remained standing. "I never should have fed them to you, or used you as a guinea pig in my experiment without your knowledge."

He shrugged and stretched his arms along the back of the sofa. "The candies didn't affect me in any way."

"No, but the intent was definitely there on my part, and it was wrong."

He didn't disagree.

She shifted on her sandaled feet and continued. "You know about my past and those insecurities played a big part in my decision to feed you my candies, as a way of protecting my emotions. It was like a big fantasy for me, being ravished without having any expectations of you at all because you were under the influence of an aphrodisiac."

He continued to stare at her, looking as though he wanted to argue those points, but refraining from commenting in order to hear her out.

Pacing to the other end of the sofa, she forced herself to relax, but it was a difficult feat when she had no idea how all this would end. "In the beginning I told myself your passion wasn't real, that it was all a product of a stimulant, and because of that I was able to convince myself that I'd avoid getting hurt when our affair ended because I wouldn't be emotionally involved with you.

"But every time we were together I wanted what we shared to be real. It *felt* real, and that scared me because I knew I was falling for you. Then I started to question whether your feelings for me were genuine, or a product of the aphrodisiac." She glanced at him and absently tugged on her lower lip with her teeth. "There was also a part of me that just couldn't believe that someone like you could want someone like me beyond a brief fling."

He moved off the couch and came toward her, his stride purposeful. When he reached her, he gently framed her face in his big hands, the intensity in his bright blue eyes holding her gaze hostage.

"Kayla, I wanted you from the first moment I met you at the Commerce dinner. Your smile, your eyes, your laughter, your curvy body...everything about you drew me in. And then I really got to know you, who you are *inside*, and that's when I fell in love with you."

She put her forehead to his, knowing she'd never get tired of him saying those words. Her chest expanded with so much emotion it felt as though it might burst.

It was time for her to bare what was in her heart, too.

A smile trembled on her lips. "I love you, too, Jack."

"Thank God!"

He wrapped his arms around her, pulled her close, and Kayla felt her aching heart mend itself and her insecurities fade into the past, where they belonged. This was her future, here with Jack. Secure in his embrace, there was no room for doubts or uncertainties. She felt adored. Cherished. Loved.

There was only one thing left for her to do.

She would bare her body to the man she wanted to spend the rest of her life with.

"Take me to your bedroom, Jack," she whispered in his ear.

A teasing, tempting grin tipped the corner of his sexy mouth. "What, no feeding me candies this time?"

"Nope." She'd given her plan for those candies a lot of thought and came up with an alternate idea she was happy with. "I had to scrap my idea for aphrodisiac candies, but I decided I'm going to sell them at Pure Indulgence without the stimulant. I think they'll inspire lustful thoughts because of what the candies resemble, not necessarily because of what's inside of them."

"That's a great idea," he agreed.

She nipped playfully at his chin. "From now on, between you and me, it's nothing but the real thing. Real desire. Real passion."

A groan rumbled up from his chest. "I like the sound of that."

He led her up the darkened stairs into an equally shadowed master bedroom. He didn't attempt to turn on the light, so she did, illuminating the room so that there was nowhere to hide. Jack didn't say a word, but the initial surprise she saw etching his features spoke volumes—he hadn't expected her to be so bold, so brave.

But the anticipation glowing hot and bright in his eyes emboldened her, made her feel feminine and seductive. This man had helped her find the sensual woman lost inside the body her mother and Doug had criticized...and Kayla liked the wanton she was beginning to discover in herself with Jack.

"I want you to see the real me," she whispered, and pushed him back until he was sitting on the mattress, an avid audience of one for her strip show. "*All* of me."

Standing in front of him, less than a foot away so he could touch if he wanted to, she began unbuttoning the bodice of her dress, until the material parted and she was able to shrug it off her shoulders and down her arms. This unveiling was as much for her as it was for him. A final shedding of that last lingering bit of insecurity that had no place between her and Jack.

He watched as she shimmied the skirt of the dress over her hips, then let it drop to the floor at her feet, leaving her clad in her prettiest lingerie—a sheer lace bra and matching panties in a deep plum shade.

She let him look his fill, and he did so hungrily, and with so much heat in his eyes that she felt seared everywhere he gazed.

"Take off your bra, sweetheart," he urged huskily.

It was gone in less than thirty seconds, her full, lush breasts spilling free right at Jack's eye level. Her nipples puckered into tight, hard points that begged for the touch of his tongue, the wet suction of his mouth.

"You are so perfect," he murmured, and spread his thighs wider apart. "Come closer," he urged.

She stepped between his legs, until his knees bracketed her thighs and that wicked, wonderful mouth of his was an excruciating inch away from her breasts. She could feel his warm, damp breath blowing across her nipples, and she trembled with need.

Then his fingers trailed up the back of her thighs, and she began to quiver all over as he began a slow, thorough exploration of her body—skimming his palms along every curve, every dip and every soft, rounded swell that defined her voluptuous figure.

She would have been lying if she said she was completely at ease standing half-naked in front of him, all her physical flaws and imperfections on display. But when his tongue lapped at her breast, circled a nipple, and she arched her back and moaned shamelessly for more, the rest of her doubts evaporated. Everywhere he touched and caressed he gave her such immense pleasure she forgot why she'd ever been modest with him.

She twined her fingers through his soft, thick hair as he continued to suckle her breast. She felt him tug the waistband of her panties off her hips, then pushed them down her legs and off. Completely naked now, he nudged her legs apart with his foot, and she gasped as his long fingers slid between her thighs, unerringly finding the exact spot that could quickly send her soaring over the edge of a hot, clenching orgasm.

His mouth left her breasts and traversed lower, his lips skimming over her soft belly...her mons...and then his tongue joined the slow slide of his thumb against her cleft.

"Jack..." she rasped.

He tipped his head back, his jaw clenched tight and his eyes hot and demanding. "Let me watch you when you come."

She nodded knowing it was all part of everything that was real between them tonight. Three strokes later she gave him what he'd asked for...let him watch as her climax shuddered through her. It robbed her of breath and the ability to stand on her shaking legs when it was finally over.

Next thing she knew, she was lying on a soft bedspread and he was moving over her, between her thighs. He braced his forearms on either side of her head so she was able to look into his eyes. She lifted her knees so that their hips met and the heated length of his shaft brushed intimately against her.

A private smile curved her lips.

"What are you grinning about?" he asked.

She ran her hands down his muscled back, over his buttocks, and pulled him closer so that he was nearly penetrating her. "You're thrilled to see me." Finally, the reaction she'd hoped for since he'd greeted her at the door.

"Hell yeah, I am," he growled, and proved it by sliding deep inside her. Then he began to move at a slow, leisurely pace. "I'm even more thrilled to have you in my bed, right where you belong. I may never let you out of it."

"Sounds lovely," she said on a wistful sigh. "But we both have businesses to run."

"Then how about you marry me and then I know you'll be in my bed every night for the rest of my life?" he suggested.

She went still and looked up at Jack, not doubting for a second the sincerity of his proposal, or his love for her. "Yes," she whispered around the joy filling her heart. "Yes, I'll marry you."

He looked immensely pleased with himself. "And what about filling up this big house with kids?" he asked, rolling his hips lazily against hers. "You up for that task?"

"Oh, yeah," she purred, imagining a little boy or girl with their father's blue eyes and being spoiled rotten by their aunt Jillian. "Especially if it means lots and lots of practicing beforehand."

"You got it, but you have to promise me two things," he said, as his thrusts deepened.

That sweet tension began to build again, and Kayla

struggled to keep her mind on their conversation. "Anything at all."

"Promise me *I'll* be your main indulgence other than chocolate." He winked. "And no more funny stuff with your desserts."

She laughed, then groaned as another flex of his hips brought her that much closer to another breath-stealing climax. "You've got yourself a deal."

"And you, Kayla Thomas, have yourself a husband."

Then all talking ceased as they both gave in to the desire and passion that was theirs, and theirs alone.

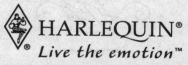

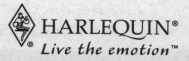

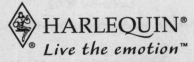

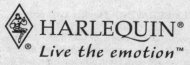

COMING NEXT MONTH

#949 IT'S ALL ABOUT EVE Tracy Kelleher
When tap pants go missing not once, but *three* times, lingerie-store owner Eve Cantoro calls in the cops. As soon as Carter Moran arrives, he hopes Eve will keep calling, and often! The chemistry between them is red-hot, and as events heat up at the shop, Eve's stock isn't the only lingerie that goes missing....

#950 UNDER FIRE Jamie Denton
Some Like It Hot, Bk. 3
OSHA investigator Jana Linney has never had really *good* sex. So when she meets sexy firefighter Ben Perry, she decides to do something about it. Having a one-night stand isn't like her, but if anyone can "help" her, Ben can. Only, one night isn't enough... and a repeat performance is unlikely, once Jana discovers she's investigating the death of one of Ben's co-workers. Still, now that Jana's tasted what sex *should* be, she's *not* giving it up....

#951 ONE NAUGHTY NIGHT Joanne Rock
The Wrong Bed—linked to Single in South Beach
Renzo Cesare has always been protective toward women. So it makes complete sense for him to "save" the beautiful but obviously out of her league Esmerelda Giles at a local nightclub. But it doesn't make sense for him to claim to be her blind date. He's not sure where *that* impulse came from. But before he can figure out a way to tell her the truth, she's got him in a lip lock so hot, he'll say anything to stay there!

#952 BARELY BEHAVING Jennifer LaBrecque
Heat
After three dead-end trips down the matrimonial highway, Tammy Cooper is giving up on marriage. She's the town bad girl—and she's proud of it. From now on, her motto is "Love 'em and leave 'em." Only, her plan takes a hit when gorgeous veterinarian Niall Fortson moves in next door. He's more than willing to let Tammy love him all she wants. But he's not letting her go anywhere....

HTCNM1003